of
Essay Writing

By the same author

Little Red Book Series

Little Red Book of Slang-Chat Room Slang

Little Red Book of English Vocabulary Today

Little Red Book of Grammar Made Easy

Little Red Book of English Proverbs

Little Red Book of Prepositions

Little Red Book of Idioms and Phrases

Little Red Book of Euphemisms

Little Red Book of Effective Speaking Skills

Little Red Book of Modern Writing skills

Little Red Book of Verbal Phrases

Little Red Book of Synonyms

Little Red Book of Antonyms

Little Red Book of Common Errors

Little Red Book of Letter Writing

Little Red Book of Perfect Written English

Little Red Book of Punctuation

A2Z Book Series

A2Z Quiz Book

A2Z Book of Word Origins

Others

The Book of Fun Facts

The Book of More Fun Facts

The Book of Firsts and Lasts

The Book of Virtues

The Book of Motivation

Read Write Right: Common Errors in English

The Students'Companion

Fiction

Vilayti Pani: The Anglo-Indian Novel

Little Red Book *of* Essay Writing

Terry O'Brien

RUPA

First published in 2012 by
Rupa Publications India Pvt. Ltd.
7/16, Ansari Road, Daryaganj
New Delhi 110002

Sales centres:
Allahabad Bengaluru Chennai
Hyderabad Jaipur Kathmandu
Kolkata Mumbai

Copyright © Terry O'Brien 2012

First impression 2012

All rights reserved.
No part of this publication may be reproduced, transmitted,
or stored in a retrieval system, in any form or by any means,
electronic, mechanical, photocopying, recording or otherwise,
without the prior permission of the publisher.

ISBN: 978-81-291-2055-7

10 9 8 7 6 5 4 3 2 1

Terry O'Brien asserts the moral right to be identified
as the author of this work.

Printed in India by
HT Media Ltd.
B-2, Sector 63
Noida 201307

This book is sold subject to the condition that it shall not,
by way of trade or otherwise, be lent, resold, hired out, or
otherwise circulated, without the publisher's prior consent,
in any form of binding or cover other than that
in which it is published.

*I dedicate this book to late Prof. A.P. O'Brien,
my father, friend, guide and mentor, who
inspired me to the canon of excellence:
re-imagining what's essential*

PREFACE

The word *essay* derives from the French infinitive *essayer*, "to try" or "to attempt". In English *essay* first meant "a trial" or "an attempt", and this is still an alternative meaning. The Frenchman Michel de Montaigne (1533–1592) was the first author to describe his work as essays; he used the term to characterise these as "attempts" to put his thoughts into writing, and his essays grew out of his commonplacing. The essay is a piece of writing which is often written from an author's personal point of view. Essays can consist of a number of elements, including:literary criticism, political manifestos, learned arguments, observations of daily life, recollections, and reflections of the author. The definition of an essay is vague, overlapping with those of an article and a short story.

In some countries (e.g., the United States and Canada and India), essays have become a major part of formal education. Secondary students are taught structured essay formats to improve their writing skills. The admission essays are often used by universities in selecting applicants and, in the humanities and social sciences, as a way of assessing the performance of students during final exams. The concept of an "essay" has been extended to other mediums beyond writing.

An essay has been defined in a variety of ways. One definition is a "prose composition with a focused subject of discussion" or a "long, systematic discourse". It is difficult

viii *Preface*

to define the genre into which essays fall. Aldous Huxley, a leading essayist, gives guidance on the subject. He notes that "like the novel, the essay is a literary device" for saying almost everything about almost anything, usually on a certain topic.

By tradition, almost by definition, the essay is a short piece, and it is therefore impossible to give all things full play within the limits of a single essay.

A definition essay defines a word, term, or concept in depth by providing a personal commentary on what the specific subject means.

A. Most physical objects have a definition about which most people agree.
   1. Most people will agree on what trees, windows, computers, and pencils are in general.
B. However, abstract terms, such as *love, pain,* or *patriotism,* have different meanings for different individuals since such terms play on people's feelings more than their physical senses.
C. The definition essay provides a personal, extended definition of such terms by linking or comparing the term to a previous definition and by illustrating how that term should be applied.

'A good essay must have this permanent quality about it; it must draw its curtain round us, but it must be a curtain that shuts us in not out.'
Virginia Woolf

'Undoubtedly, the point of the essay is to change things.'
Edward Tufte

Essay Writing

The Six P'S

WRITING your essays try to achieve the **six P's:**
- Pleasant Appearance
- Proper Selection of Subject
- Planning
- Proportion
- Perspicuity
- Persuasiveness.

1. Pleasant Appearance

☞ Do write legibly and without crossingsout.
☞ Penmanship is important.
☞ Do indent for every paragraph, including the first. ("To indent" means to make the first line shorter than the others by leaving a space at the beginning of it.)
☞ Do keep a left-hand margin, and try to keep a right-hand one too, making this as even as possible, for a jagged ending of lines looks most unattractive.

2. Proper Selection of Subject

In examinations candidates are usually allowed a fairly wide choice of essay subject.
☞ Choose one that suits you.

Remember that there are roughly **five types of essays**:
1. Narrative
2. Descriptive
3. Reflective
4. Argumentative
5. Expository

2 *Little Red Book of Essay Writing*

☞ Find out which kinds you can do best.
☞ Don't plunge into discussions of scientific and technical subjects without a detailed knowledge.
☞ Don't attempt artistic description if you are deficient in imagination.
☞ Don't choose vast general subjects like " Colour" or " Truth" "Liberty" unless you can decide quickly which particular aspects you want to deal with.
☞ Be sure to read the titles carefully and notice any qualifying words or unusual expressions. If you don't quite understand a quotation or proverb set as a title, or feel there is some ambiguity about it, don't choose it.
☞ Make sure you understand the meaning of your title perfectly.
☞ Having once selected your subject, abide by your choice.

3. Planning

The four essential stages in the creation of an essay are:
☞ Thinking   ☞ Arranging
☞ Writing   ☞ Revising

NOTE:
☞ Always have rough paper.
☞ Write your ideas down on this paper first.
☞ Always make a plan (a general outline or scheme, a skeleton framework).
☞ Don't sit thinking too long; get your ideas down on paper quickly.
☞ Plan your time too and practice writing to time-limits. (Spend, say, $\frac{1}{6}$ of the time allowed on thinking about it and drawing up your outline, $\frac{3}{4}$ of the time on writing it, and $\frac{1}{12}$ of the time for revision and correction.)

Little Red Book of Essay Writing   **3**

☞ It is important to keep enough time for a final reading, but be careful not to have too much time left over or you will be tempted to add on afterthoughts to an essay already finished and revised.

4. Proportion

The essay must have:

☞ Beginning   ☞ Middle   ☞ End

Make a good introduction:

☞ Not too lengthy or you will exhaust your theme in the opening paragraph
☞ Follow it up, developing your subject
☞ Round off with a satisfactory conclusion—not ending abruptly in mid-air, or tamely on a minor point.

Pay attention to the **architecture of composition:**

☞ Good paragraphing is vital
☞ Break up your essay into paragraphs, following your rough plan
☞ An unbroken, un-paragraphed page is most boring for your examiner
☞ On the other hand, don't chop up too finely—the modern journalistic habit of severing up single sentences as paragraphs is not to be imitated.
☞ Vary the length of your paragraphs—a short **"sandwich paragraph"** between two longer ones can be very effective.
☞ Arrange your paragraphs properly—don't skip backwards and forwards.
☞ Each idea should follow on in logical order, each paragraph advancing your essay and the succession of paragraphs corresponding with the sense, so that any alteration in the order of paragraphs would dislocate the whole unity of the essay.

4 *Little Red Book of Essay Writing*

5. Perspicuity

- ☞ Don't mess and muddle
- ☞ Get your thoughts straight 'before' you write
- ☞ Be lucid and clear
- ☞ Perspicuity implies simplicity, brevity and precision.
- ☞ Write in direct and plain English.
- ☞ Write with economy and accuracy, for perspicuity, like that other great virtue in writing, sincerity, implies "saying what you mean, and meaning what you say, — using no words that you do not understand, measuring your epithets, never repeating phrases from books without due consideration, never writing a sentence for the sound rather than the sensed " (Fowler)

6. Persuasiveness

To charm your reader or examiner your writing must be-
- ☞ Not stale but fresh
- ☞ Not trite but original
- ☞ Not wooden but lively and imaginative
- ☞ Not monotonous but varied
- ☞ Not spineless but vigorous
- ☞ Not faded but vivid
- ☞ Use concrete and specific images, not abstract and general ones
- ☞ Appeal to the senses of sight, sound, smell, taste and touch
- ☞ Use similes, metaphors and other figures of speech to stimulate the reader's imagination — in short, study suitable interest devices to attract, impress and hold the attention

Little Red Book of Essay Writing **5**

Approaches for Writing Different Types of Essays

1. Narrative

☞ Historical events   ☞ Legends
☞ Incidents   ☞ Stories
☞ Short biographies

Purpose

☞ To tell convincingly a series of real, or imaginary events
☞ Keep the thread of your story
☞ Present your facts in correct sequence and don't, digress.
☞ Don't obtrude your own opinions too much, and keep your reflections to the end.
☞ Don't mix your tenses, and don't be tempted to use the Historic Present: this, although common in many languages, seldom sounds natural in English.
☞ Give a feeling of movement to your story.
☞ Introduce dramatic interest, devices of suspense in a historical subject, Historical parallels to enliven the subject

Suggested Outline for an Historical Event:

(1) Introduction:Date Place People Occasion.
(2) Circumstances: Incidents.
(3) Results.
(4) Reflections and Conclusions

A Biography

(1) Introduction: Early life Parentage Surroundings Education
(2) Career. Rise to power. Most famous works
(3) Last years
(4) Conclusion. Character Influence

6 *Little Red Book of Essay Writing*

2. Descriptive

Animals, plants, minerals, places, people.

Purpose: To give a picture.

> *NOTE:* Distinguish between two types of description:
> (a) Scientific: Accurate like a photograph.
> (b) Artistic: Imaginative like a painting.
> ☞ Give a general impression first, then fill in with vivid details.
> ☞ Think and write in terms of colours, sounds, smells, tastes, shapes, sizes, textures, heat, cold, movement, etc. Make use of Interest Devices

Outline for Animals, Plants etc.

(1) Introduction, Kind (class, order, species). Origin.
(2) Characteristics — qualities, habits, appearance.
(3) How produced or obtained.
(4) Relation to man and nature (useful, attractive, harmful, etc.).
(5) Concluding remarks.

Outline for people.

(1) Introduction: A first glimpse.
(2) Physical description.
(3) Characterization by:
   (a) incident
   (b) inference (from surroundings,, gestures, voice, what the person says, does and thinks, what others say, do and think about him).
(4) Conclusion

Reflections: For Places, e.g. a town.

(1) Introduction. General impression. Position. Size.

Little Red Book of Essay Writing **7**

(2) History
(3) Buildings of particular interest.
(4) Industries.
(5) Special features.
(6) Concluding remarks.

3. Reflective

☞ Habits
☞ Social
☞ Domestic
☞ Philosophical topics

☞ Qualities
☞ Political
☞ Moral

Purpose: To give your opinions on the subject.

NOTE: Originality and power of thought count here and the personal element is stronger than in other types of essay. Guard against ponderous and sententious moralizing- don't make your essay into a sermon.

Suggested Outline:
(1) Introduction. Definition or explanation.
(2) Working and development of theme.
(3) Value.
(4) Effects.
(5) Concluding remarks.

4. Argumentative

Subjects:
☞ Controversial
☞ Polemical
☞ Debatable subjects, often set in the form of question or quotation.

Purpose: To convince.

8 *Little Red Book of Essay Writing*

> *NOTE:* Either enumerate all the "pros" and then the "cons ", followed by your summing up and final verdict, or give the 'pros" and "cons" alternately. One method is to statethe opinion in the introduction, then bring in "scoring points", then get seriously to grips with your subject, giving reasons for and against.

☞ Don't show too much feeling, but on the other hand don't leave all feeling out.
☞ Be decisive, but be fair.
☞ Distinguish carefully between facts and opinions.
☞ Be logical and relevant or you will weaken your argument.

Suggested Outline
(1) Introduction, stating case.
(2) Scoring point. Reason one.
(3) Reasons two, three or more.
(4) Scoring point and reason one.
(5) Reasons two, three or more.
(6) Summary, Balance and Appeal.

6. Expository

☞ Institutions   ☞ Industries
☞ Occupations   ☞ Literary
☞ Scientific

Purpose: To explain.

> *NOTE:*
> ☞ Attack your problem with vigour
> ☞ Ask and answer the questions How, Why, When, Where?
> ☞ Supply all important details. (A knowledge of facts is essential here.)

Little Red Book of Essay Writing **9**

☞ Precision of language and clear presentation are vital.

Suggested Outline
(1) Introduction
(2) Definition
(3) History
(4) Explanation of the subject
(5) Results, good or bad
(6) Concluding remarks.

Some Don'ts

1. Don't number your paragraphs or give them headings (reserve this for your plan).
2. Don't use abbreviations: Examiners don't want to read about "exams" or "bikes".
3. Don't write numbers in figures but in words, except for dates and large numbers.
4. Don't use slang, unless in inverted commas, and don't use archaisms or any other objectionable styles.
5. Don't use too many quotations. Some candidates make their essays a patchwork of quotations to display the variety and depth of their learning. An Anecdote should be your salt, but I don't think quotation should be your pepper!
6. Don't have a "catalogue style". Avoid long lists.
7. Don't suffer from the disease *adjectivitis*. Shun lists of adjectives in pairs. e.g.: "A tall slim figure with beautiful black hair and plump rosy cheeks."

   Avoid unnecessary modifiers — e.g. "very", "quite", "absolutely".

10 *Little Red Book of Essay Writing*

Measure your adjectives, especially your superlatives.

8. Don't overwork "be" and "have". Instead of "she was", "it is ", etc., use more dynamic words.

9. Don't have jingles. e.g. "I was deeply impressed by that antique gold chest." Keep your rhymes for poetry, not prose.

10. Don't be someone else. Be yourself. "The chief value of an essay, both intrinsically and as a piece of training, lies in its being an expression of a bit of yourself" (Fowler)

11. Don't be flippant. Maxwell tells us: "Humour is a dangerous tool, and the examination room is not the best workshop to use it in." Attempts to be amusing in a foreign language often fall very flat.

12. Don't have a "wandering" style. In short examination essays it is vitally important to keep to the subject.

13. Don't insert apologetic statements such as ; "Time will not permit ", "the space at my disposal is too limited ", etc.

14. Don't use beginnings like: "I take up my pen to write " or " Although time allowed is short ", or "What can I say about..?" or stale and stereotyped endings like: " In conclusion we may say ", or "Finally we see that the advantages outweigh the disadvantages ", or "Thus, looking at the matter from both points of view, we may say that ", or "summing up, we can conclude that …"

It is wiser to make a good opening with an anecdote, quotation, epigram or definition, and to close with a brief summary, with comments, a striking sentence or epigram.

Little Red Book of Essay Writing **11**

Figures of Speech

Those are vivid and striking images that will enrich your writing considerably. Here is a list of some of the most important figures of speech in English. These, if correctly and imaginatively used, can help to make your style more lively and interesting.

1. Simile

This is a very common figure of speech in English. It is a comparison, showing similarity between one thing and another, and usually introduced by the word as or like:
e.g. Her tears fell like rain.
      He is as patient as a sheep.
      You look like a ghost!

Here are some idiomatic similes in common use in English:

as good as gold	as clear as crystal
as right as rain	as fit as a fiddle
as fat as butter	as heavy as lead
as thin as a rake	as light as a feather
as dry s a bone	as fresh as a daisy
as sharp as a needle	as pretty as a picture
as brave as a lion	as happy as a lark
as sound as a bell	as cool as a cucumber
as bold as brass	as busy as a bee or bees
as cold as ice	as ugly as sin
as hard as nails	as brown as a berry
as slippery as an eel	as true as steel
as hungry as a hunter	as stiff as a poker
as drunk as a lord	as dead as a door-nail
as sober as a judge	as old as the hills

12 *Little Red Book of Essay Writing*

as poor as a church mouse   as strong as a horse
as rich as Croesus   as weak as water

2. Metaphor

Here the comparison is not introduced by as or like. Instead of saying "He is as brave as a lion ", we say "He is a lion ". Instead of resemblance we have identification.

e.g. He is just a poor fish.
      Here is the fruit of my labours.
      He is a tower of strength.
      She was cut off in the flower of her youth and beauty.
      This shop is a real gold-mine.

Many metaphors are in common use in English.

a ray of hope   a flash of inspiration
the fire of passion   a flow of words
the depths of despair   the dawn of history
the heights of happiness   to bombard with questions
the school of life   to be consumed with curiosity
the wind of change   to launch a campaign
the book of nature   to steer clear of
the key to the mystery   to strike a note
the heart of the matter   to overflow with ideas
the root of the trouble   to put up a good fight
                             to burst into tears.

Warning: Don't mix your metaphors by confusing your comparisons:-.

e.g. Life is not always a bed of roses.it is sometimes stormy. (A flower-bed cannot become stormy!)

3. Personification

This is a form of metaphorical speech in which inanimate

Little Red Book of Essay Writing **13**

or abstract things and ideas are treated as if they were human persons. Thus we speak of time as "Father Time" or the moon as "Lady Moon" or of spring as a young girl and winter as an old man.

e.g.:

Love is blind.

Death is no respecter of persons.

The winds are whispering.

4. Contrast (Antithesis)

This is the opposite of metaphor. By balancing two opposing words or ideas .against each other a vivid sense of contrast and difference is obtained.

e.g.:

- Speech is silver; silence is golden.
- To err is human ; to forgive, divine.
- He was a good husband but a bad father.
- God made the country and man made the town.

5. Paradox

This is also a form of contrast—the presentation of truth in a form apparently self-contradictory and absurd.

e.g.:

- Only the man who has known fear can be truly brave. We must die in order to live.
- "Vision is the art of seeing things invisible " (Swift).

6. Oxymoron

Here the contrast is sharper and the contradictory words are put as close together as possible. It is a kind of condensed paradox.

14 *Little Red Book of Essay Writing*

e.g.:
- a wise fool
- an open secret
- a cheerful pessimist.
- a living death
- bitter-sweet memories.
- the kind cruelty of the surgeon's knife.

7. Epigram

This is a short witty saying, often containing a paradoxical idea.

e.g.:
- "Fools rush in where angels fear to tread." (Pope)
- "The child is father of the man." (Wordsworth)
- "A favourite has no friend." (Gray)

8. Transferred Epithet

This is an adjective placed before a word to which it does not really apply.

e.g.:

"The ploughman plods his weary way."
(Gray)
(The ploughman is weary, not the way.)

Transferred epithets are found in such phrases as:

a sleepless night	the condemned cell
melancholy news	a happy time
a burning question	an anxious letter

9. Exaggeration (Hyperbole)

This is the use of overstatement for the sake of effect. When you say to a person " I haven't seen you for ages"

Little Red Book of Essay Writing **15**

you don't really mean "ages", and when you say "He ran like the wind" you don't seriously think that he was as fast as the wind — you are merely exaggerating to make a vivid impression.

e.g.:

- ♦ I've heard that joke hundreds of times.
- ♦ I thought that I would die of laughing.
- ♦ It's so cold and we are absolutely frozen!
- ♦ "All the perfumes of Arabia will not sweeten this little hand." (Shakespeare.)

10. Understatement

There are two main kinds of understatement.

(i) One is when we try to soften unpleasant things, e.g. by calling death "sleep", or a lie " an inaccuracy " This is called by the Greek word **Euphemism**.

e.g. My husband fell asleep (or passed on or passed away) last week (died).

Sometimes I think you are a stranger to the truth (a liar)

(ii) The other kind of understatement is used intentionally to give greater positive emphasis to the idea. This is called by the Greek word **Litotes**, and it is very common in English.

e.g. **Understatement**   **Real Meaning**
- ♦ not bad   = very good
- ♦ not uncommon   = very common
- ♦ not a few   = many
- ♦ not a little   = much
- ♦ quite good/rather good = excellent
- ♦ He is no coward   = He is very brave

16 *Little Red Book of Essay Writing*

11. Climax

This means "a ladder" or "series of stops" and is the presentation of a number of ideas to give a gradual increase in intensity, so that the last idea is the strongest of all.
e.g.:

- "I came, I saw, I conquered."
- "What a piece of work is man!"(How infinite in faculties! In form and motion how express and. admirable! In action how like an angel. In apprehension how like a god !) (Shakespeare)
- The child stirred; his eyes opened; he smiled and cried Mother!

12. Anti-climax

This is just the opposite: the ideas descend in order of importance. It is often used in humorous writing.
e.g.:

- He lost his wife, his children — and his purse.
- He is a great philosopher, a fine teacher and he plays tennis well too.

13. Onomatopoeia

This means simply the formation of words by the imitation of sounds. The sense echoes the sound.
e.g.:

- The buzzing of bees.
- The patter of rain.
- The sound of the cuckoo.
- The water dripped from the tap.

Bang, splash, bump, thud, swish, crack, groan, whisper, scream, hiss are all onomatopoeic words — and there are

Little Red Book of Essay Writing **17**

hundreds more. Try to make your own lists of vivid sound—words.

14. Alliteration

This is also to do with sound, and is the frequent repetition of the same letter or sound in words such as: "apt alliteration's artful aid"

e.g.:

- ◆ Pink pills for pale people.
- ◆ Stay the summer in the sunny south.

Notice how fond English people are of alliterative phrases. The taste for alliteration is very strong in the English language, and besides the alliterative similes:" good as gold", "bold as brass" and so on, we have hundreds of little alliterative phrases in everyday use.

e.g.:

chop and change	the lap of luxury
sink or swim	make or mar
part and parcel	do or die
first and foremost	fact or fiction
last but not least	spick and span
slowly but surely	hale and hearty
fast and furious	friend or foe
short and sweet	safe and sound
from top to toe	neither rhyme nor reason
through thick and thin	toss and turn
the why and wherefore	

Notice too our alliterative proverbs:

- Waste not, want not.
- A miss is as good as a mile.
- Every dog has his day.

18 *Little Red Book of Essay Writing*

- He who laughs last laughs longest.
- Look before you leap.

These are just **fourteen figures of speech.** There are several others of course such as apostrophe, synecdoche, metonymy etc.

Samples of Good Writing

1. Beginnings of Essays

- "Of Gardens": "God Almighty first planted a garden". (Francis Bacon)
- "Of Death": "Men fear death as children fear to go into the dark. " (Francis Bacon)
- "Deaths of Little Children": "A Grecian philosopher being asked why he wept for the death of his son, since the sorrow was in vain, replied, 'I weep on that account.' And his answer became his wisdom. " (Leigh Hunt)
- "Mrs. Battle's Opinions on Whist": "'A clear fire, a clean hearth, and the rigour of the game.' This was the celebrated wish of old Sarah Battle (now with God) who, next to her devotions, loved a good game at Whist." (Charles Lamb)
- "Of Manners": "Half the world, it is said, knows not how the other half lives. Our exploring expedition saw the … islanders getting their dinner off human bones; and they are said to eat their own wives and children." (R. W. Emerson)

2. Endings of Essays

- "Of Adversity": "Certainly virtue is like precious odours, most fragrant when they are incensed or crushed: for

Little Red Book of Essay Writing **19**

prosperity doth best discover vice; but adversity doth best discover virtue. " (Francis Bacon)

- "Happiness of Temper": "It is certainly a better way to oppose calamity by dissipation than to take up arms of reason or resolution to oppose it. By the first method we forget our miseries, by the last we only conceal them from others. By struggling with misfortunes we are sure to receive some wounds in the conflict. The only method to come off victorious is by running away. " (Oliver Goldsmith)

- "A Few Thoughts on Sleep": "Sleep is most graceful in an infant, soundest in one who has been tired in the open air, completest to the seaman after a hard voyage, most welcome to the mind haunted with one idea, most touching to look at in the parent that has wept, lightest in the playful child, proudest in the bride adored. " (Leigh Hunt)

- "Valentine's Day": "Good-morrow to my Valentine, sings poor Ophelia: and no better wish, hut with better auspices, we wish to all faithful lovers, who are not too wise to despise old legends, but are content to rank , themselves humble diocesans of old Bishop Valentine, and his true church." (Charles Lamb)

- "The Poet" : "That true land-lord! sea-lord! air-lord! Wherever snow falls, or water flows, or birds fly, wherever day and night meet in twilight, wherever the blue heaven is hung by clouds, or sown with stars, wherever are forms with transparent boundaries, wherever are outlets into celestial space, wherever is danger,. . .and awe and love, there is Beauty, plenteous as rain, shed for thee, and though thou shouldest walk the world over, thou shalt not, be able to find a condition inopportune or ignoble." (R. W. Emerson)

20 *Little Red Book of Essay Writing*

3. Interest Devices

(a) The Appeal to the Senses

Sight: "I see and feel the soft firelight warming me, playing on my silk dress, and fitfully showing me my own young figure in a glass; I see the moon of a calm winter night float full, clear, and cold, over the inky mass: of shiubbery, and the silvered turf of my grounds. " (Charlotte Bronte)

Sound: "Those who are in the habit of remarking to such matters must have noticed the passive quiet of an English landscape on Sunday. The clacking of the mill, the regularly recurring stroke of the flail, the din of the blacksmith's hammer, the whistling of the ploughman, the rattling of the cart, and all other sounds of rural labour are suspended. The very arm of dogs bark less frequently, being less disturbed by passing travellers. At such times I have almost fancied the winds sunk into quiet." (Washington Irving)

Touch: "Who has not felt the beauty of a woman's arm? — the unspeakable suggestions of tenderness that lie in the dimpled elbow, and all the varied gently-lessening curves, down to the delicate wrist, with its tiniest, almost imperceptible nicks in the firm softness. A woman's arm touched the soul of a great sculptor two thousand years ago, so that he wrought an image of it for the Parthenon which moves us still as it clasps lovingly the time-worn marble of a headless trunk. Maggie's was such an arm as that — and it had the warm tints of life." (George Eliot)

Taste: "There is no flavour comparable, I will contend, to that of the crisp, tawny, well-watched, not over-roasted, crackling, as it is well called — the very teeth are invited to their share of the pleasure at this banquet in overcoming the coy, brittle resistance... " (Charles Lamb)

Little Red Book of Essay Writing **21**

Smell. "Hallo! A great deal of steam! The pudding was out of the copper. A smell like a washing-day! That was the cloth. A smell like an eating-house and a pastry-cook's next door to each other, with a laundress's next door to that. That was the pudding." (Charles Dickens)

(b) The Appeal to the Feelings

Feeling of Shock: " Every feature quivered under the invisible cutting hand of cruel experience. In those last sharp moments of introspection she had gained such a knowledge of suffering that a fire seemed to have consumed her vision of life, reducing it to a frightful desert of eternal woe and unavailing sacrifice."

(John Oliver Hobbes)

Feeling of Movement "And every furrow heaved and bubbled, and out of every clod arose a man. Out of the earth they rose by thousands each clad from head to foot in steel, and drew their swords and rushed on Jason, where he stood in the amidst alone." (Charles Kingsley)

Feeling of cold. "(He) entered the icy water.. It made, him gasp 'and almost shriek with the cold. It froze his marrow. 'I shall die,' he cried, 'I shall die; but' better this than fire eternal."

"And so next day he was so stiff in all his joints he could not move, and he seemed one great ache. And even in sleep he felt that his very bones were like so many raging teeth." (Charles Reade)

Feeling of Heat: "The heat was so intense that the paint on the houses over against the prison parched and cracked up, and swelling into boils as it were from excess of torture, broke and crumbled away." (Charles Dickens)

22   *Little Red Book of Essay Writing*

Feeling of Terror: "At this moment a light gleamed on the wall . . . while I gazed it glided up to the ceiling and quivered over my head prepared as my mind was for horror, shaken as my nerves were by agitation, I thought the swift-darting beam was a herald of some coming vision from another world. My heart beat quick, my head grew hot; a sound filled my ears, which I deemed the rushing of wings : something seemed near me; I was oppressed, suffocated : endurance broke down, I rushed to the door and shook the lock in desperate effort." (Charlotte Bronte)

Feeling of Gloom: "The faithful chambers seem, as it were, to mourn the absence of their masters. The turkey carpet has rolled itself up, and retired sulkily under the side-board: the pictures have hidden their faces behind old sheets, of brown paper: the window-curtains have disappeared under all sorts of shabby brown envelopes: the marble bust of Sir Walpole Crawley is looking from its black corner at the oiled fire-irons, and the empty racks over the mantelpiece." (William Makepeace Thackeray.)

Feeling of Calm: "It was in the month of August, some six or seven years ago, that a traveller on foot, touched, as he emerged from a dark wood, by the beauty of the scene, threw himself under the shade of a spreading tree, and stretched his limbs on the turf for enjoyment rather than repose. The sky was deep coloured and without a cloud, save here and there a minute sultry burnished vapour, almost as glossy as the heavens. Everything was still as it was bright; all seemed brooding and basking; the bee upon its wing was the only stirring sight and its song the only sound." (Benjamin Disraeli)

Little Red Book of Essay Writing **23**

(c) Striking Figures of Speech

- "Some books are to be tasted, others swallowed, and some few to be chewed and digested." (Francis Bacon)
- "Such laughter, like sunshine on the deep sea, is very beautiful to inc." (Thomas Carlyle)
- "Every drop of ink in my pen ran cold." (Horace Walpole)
- "Her face is like a squeezed orange." (Ben Jonson)
- "A sleek, smooth, silky, soft-spoken person." (Mary Russell Mitford)
- "I do not consult physicians for I hope to die without them." (Sir William Temple)
- "The walls, like a large map, seem to be portioned and Cut into capes, seas and promontories by the various colours by which the damps have stained them." (William Cowper)
- "Youth is a blunder; manhood a struggle; old age a regret."(Benjamin Disraeli)
- "Horrid as a murderer's dream." (Dr. Johnson)
- "Discussing the character and foibles of common friends is a great sweetener and cement of friendship." (William Hazlitt)
- "I have no relish for the country: it is a kind of healthy grave." (Sydney Smith)
- "He (Tennyson) could not think up to the height of his own towering style?" (G. K. Chesterton)
- "The weather is raw and boisterous in winter, shifty and uncongenial in summer, and a downright meteorological purgatory in the spring." (Robert Louis Stevenson)
- "They that sow in tears shall reap in joy." (Psalmist)
- "After life's fitful fever he sleeps well." (Shakespeare)
- "The golden rule is that there are no golden rules." (G.B. Shaw)

24 *Little Red Book of Essay Writing*

(d) Challenging Statement:

"The reason why so few good books are written js that so few people that can write know anything." (Walter Bagehot)

(e) Effective Repetition.

"It was a sweet view sweet to the eye and the mind: English verdure, English culture, English comfort, seen under a sun bright without being oppressive"(Jane Austen)

(f) Quotation and Lively Comment

"All men are liars,' said the Psalmist; but not all liars are men." (Anon)

(g) Clever Use of Contrast

"It was a clear steel-blue day. The firmaments of air and sea were hardly separable in that all-pervading azure; only, the pensive air was pure and soft, with a woman's look, and the robust and man-like sea heaved with tong, strong, lingering swells, as Samson's chest in sleep.

Hither and thither, on high, glided the snow-white wings of small, unspeckled birds; these were the gentle thoughts of the feminine air; but to and fro in the deeps, far down in the bottomless blue, rushed. mighty leviathans, swordfish and sharks; and these were the strong, troubled, murderous thinkings of the masculine sea." (Herman Melville)

(h) Vivid Cataloguing

"Articles now considered necessities were luxuries to our forefathers, or entirely non-existent. Thus they lived without sugar till the thirteenth century; without coal till the fourteenth; without butter on their bread to the fifteenth, without tea, coffee, and soap till the seventeenth: without

Little Red Book of Essay Writing **25**

umbrellas, lamps, and pudding till the eighteenth; without trains, telegrams, gas, matches, and chloroform till the nineteenth." (CM. B. Synge)

(1) Animated Dialogue

"'I'll stake the young gentleman a crown' says the Lord Mohun's Captain.

'I thought crowns were rather scarce with the gentlemen of the army,' says Harry.

'Do they birch at college?' says the Captain.

'They birch fools,' says Harry, 'and they cafe bullies, and they fling puppies into the water.'

'Faith, then, there's some escapes drowning,' says the Captain, who was an Irishman; and all the gentlemen began to laugh, and made poor Harry only more angry." (William Makepeace Thackeray)

Some Subjects for Essays

1. Narrative

1. A journey by train.
2. A ghost story.
3. My favourite summer holiday.
4. A visit to the Taj.
5. A bad dream.
6. An uninvited guest.
7. A visit to the theatre.
8. An adventure with a wild animal.
9. A day in bed.
10. A famous battle.
11. The career of a king or queen in Indian history.

26 *Little Red Book of Essay Writing*

12. My first interview for a job.
13. An account of a walking or a cycling tour.
14. An excursion.
15. The street fight.
16. The most tiring day of my life.
17. The first ten minutes of a party.
18. A night out of doors.
19. The story of one of Shakespeare's plays.
20. The adventures of a new car-owner.

2. Descriptive

21. The sun.
22. A rainy day.
23. Dolls.
24. Those people next door.
25. The historical personage whom you would most like to have met.
26. Monkeys.
27. A quarrelsome man.
28. Snake-charmers.
29. College elections.
30. A true friend.
31. Travelling in an aeroplane.
32. Birds.
33. Simple pleasures.
34. Earthquakes.
35. Things one cannot get rid of.
36. Indian beggars.
37. An ideal home.
38. A village.
39. My favourite book.
40. Ships and boats.

Little Red Book of Essay Writing **27**

3. Reflective

41. What makes a good businessman?
42. Heroism in everyday life.
43. Fashion.
44. Superstition.
45. Education : its meaning and purpose.
46. Punctuality.
47. Ambition.
48. The choice of a profession.
49. Community projects.
50. "The paths of glory lead but to the grave."
51. Colour
52. If I had a thousand rupees.
53. The relative advantages of health, wealth and wisdom.
54. Examinations.
55. Cleanliness.
56. The pleasures of hope.
57. Flying kites.
58. Hero worship.
59. "Knowledge is power."
60. Sport.

4. Argumentative

61. The evils and benefits of competition.
62. Is popularity a criterion of merit?
63. Co-education.
64. Science and religion.
65. Novel-reading is a waste of time.
66. Dangers of communalism.
67. Are millionaires a danger or a benefit to the community?

28 *Little Red Book of Essay Writing*

68. Should people have secrets?
69. Women and careers.
70. "It is more profitable to read one man than ten books."
71. Are scientific inventions and labor-saving devices making us happier and more contented?
72. "There are falsehoods which are not lies."
73. Are proverbs a safe guide to conduct?
74. The uses and abuses of advertisement.
75. "Manners Maketh Man."
76. Should corporal punishment in schools be abolished?
77. Democracy versus dictatorship.
78. Examinations.
79. Is the system of "tipping" morally defensible?
80. Liberty cannot exist without discipline.

5. Expository

81. The management and care of a dog or horse.
82. Photography as an aid to science.
83. The game of football.
84. The work of a farmer.
85. The uses of electricity.
86. International disarmament.
87. Public schools.
88. International exhibitions.
89. Slavery in modern times.
90. My favourite hobby.
91. Forecasting the weather.
92. The future of aviation.
93. Flattery as a fine art.
94. Arctic exploration.
95. Wonders and uses of the microscope.
96. Student indiscipline.

97. Ancient and modern warfare.
98. Autobiographies.
99. Printing.
100. Strikes.

The Purpose of Your Essay

Decide what you have to say, who your audience is, and then how to communicate it.

Who What and How

To write anything — not just essays — you must first decide on:

☞ **the purpose**, which includes being quite clear about who you are talking to. Then you must decide on what you have to say

☞ **the content**; then how you will shape it — the structure.

☞ **the kind of language** you use — the style. Under style we can include presentation: whether to write it by hand or word-process it, and how to lay it out on the page.

The Process

A piece of writing, then, can be conveniently described under four headings:

> **P** for the **PURPOSE**
> **C** for the **CONTENT**
> **S** for the **STRUCTURE**
> **S** for the **STYLE**

The advantage of using the code-word **PROCESS** is that it puts purpose first.

What does your reader need to know?

30 *Little Red Book of Essay Writing*

If your partner is unknowingly heading for the edge as you walk along a clifftop, would you choose that moment to discuss the view, or ask who should be invited to your sister's wedding?

Yet written communications often ignore what the reader needs to know, concentrating instead on what the writer wants to say.

Indentifiying your Purpose as A Writer

Comparing the techniques needed for different kinds of writing, and practising them, improves writing skills for any purpose. We all have important kinds of writing to do in the course of our lives.

Practising these skills (writing a letter rather than telephoning, for example) will make it easier to write essays.

Writing essays will prepare us for other writing tasks in our future careers.

Comparing the purposes of different kinds of writing will help to make the purpose of the essay clearer by putting it into perspective.

Writing personal letters

The personal letter may have various purposes and may be loose and rambling. It is often a substitute for conversation, discussing matters of interest only to the sender and recipient. It may contain private references to shared experience that would not be understood by anyone else. But writing letters encourages your ideas to flow readily, a crucial requirement for a good essay. In any case there are more formal varieties of letters, which appear among the creative essay choices in exam papers. Their main purpose is to let you show that you can communicate effectively, with less emphasis on knowledge or structure.

For example:

A friend is thinking of trying to take up a career in music and, has written to you asking for advice. Write a letter in reply which does not discourage your friend, but makes clear the difficulties and challenges to be faced.

Some of these letters are based on extracts from literature and journalism, which you have to read first.

Writing business letters

These have a specific purpose: to inform, order or sell, so that the sender's business will benefit. Anything irrelevant to its purpose will work against it. A letter asking for a long-standing bill to be paid, after many previous letters and phone calls, will refer to possible legal action rather than inject humour with an apt quotation from Shakespeare.

Writing a business or investigative report

This has its purpose clearly stated, in relation to the content and the readers aimed at. The purpose is the essential part of what is usually titled the Introduction. It may be given the title *Terms of Reference*. The 'terms' are the reasons for the investigation, the situation or problem, the audience, and what action, if any, they are expected or advised to take. The Introduction may include a Summary and Conclusions.

The straightforward patterns and style of such reports work well for certain kinds of essays, especially in the sciences. The outlines of an essay and an investigative report on a similar theme are placed side by side for comparison.

The newspaper report

This aims to state as concisely and objectively as possible the

Who	Where	Why
What	When	How

32 *Little Red Book of Essay Writing*

of any event considered newsworthy, bearing in mind the readership of the publication. This **'Five-Ws-plus-How'** formula is a useful reminder of the questions that any piece of writing may be required to answer, including business-style reports and essays, in which we shall see it at work.

The newspaper reporter also aims to be readable, but *clarity is more important.* The essence of the news report is often put first, with less important facts filling it out.

The feature articles of newspapers and magazines

These have various purposes. What they have in common is the aim to:

inform	**explain**	**entertain**
comment	**persuade**	

The personal column or opinion piece is akin to the creative essay of the schoolroom. The following topic, and many similar ones, have been the subject matter of many a column:

'Modern gadgets!'

Give your views on the importance to everyday life of computers, cellular telephones, microwave cookers and satellite television.

The main *difference between feature articles and essays* is that the essay does not have to interest a great number of people, nor does it need to be quite so informative or up to date as the journalism. *But both articles and essays have to support opinions with fact.*

- As a model for creative essays, study how this support is given in the more subjective personal columns.
- As a model for the more academic essay, the main subject of this book, study how this support is given in articles of exposition and argument.

Little Red Book of Essay Writing **33**

Writing Essays

What is your teacher looking for?

Essays too have their own specific requirements. Tutors may provide a course outline, but check with your tutor (or examination body) if you are in any doubt. In general, your essay should show that you can:

- collect relevant information quickly and use the knowledge to focus clearly on the set topic;
- read critically and purposefully;
- analyse processes and problems and argue a case;
- relate theory to specific examples;
- make a creative contribution to the subject;
- structure the material logically and express it clearly.

Although clarity in essays is more in demand than readability (except for the more creative ones), put yourself in the place of a tutor or examiner who has to wade through a hundred or so in a week. Make your essay as readable as possible without straining for effect. The best journalism will provide models for this quality too.

Letters, reports and articles are often asked for in the 'composition' section of secondary school exams rather than 'essays', and coursework projects take these and other forms.

Vicky struggles with his plan

Looking over his essay on *'How to lose weight and keep it lost'* for his foundation course, Vicky's head was spinning, It was 2,000 words long. He had not made a plan of it because it had all been clear in his head. Now he saw that he had lost his way in the middle. He made a plan of the structure that

34 *Little Red Book of Essay Writing*

he found. The five steps for losing weight were first listed, which was a great help:

1. Decide exactly how much weight you want to lose.
2. Take actions to achieve it.
3. Analyse results of actions.
4. Continue actions if succeeding, or try other methods.
5. Among other methods, find someone who has achieved success and follow that example.

The main problem was step 2. This divided into actions in general: first, become interested in your health; secondly, find out where your diet is going wrong; thirdly, get excited about losing weight — take the pleasure rather than the pain. Then there were three specific actions, but it was not clear to what general action they referred — all or the last. The third specific action was followed, with no link, to: 'Perhaps you have problem food.' There was a three-step procedure for cracking this type of problem. Step one was to get leverage. Then there were two steps to achieve leverage...

Vicky asked his tutor how to deal with this.

Tutor comment

'First of all, this is a report rather than an essay, isn't it?' said the tutor. 'I would have advised you to use plenty of headings and bullet points, to avoid this confusing repetition of "steps" and "stages" and "actions". Use "steps" for the five main sections only. Avoid "stages" and keep to "methods", not "actions".

'Your section 2 needs restructuring. This is really the body of the essay. The five points of the procedure should, I think, be the introduction, to explain the whole thing. Then

Little Red Book of Essay Writing **35**

go through the different operations without dividing them further, in the best order. Make sure you link each operation to the next, showing the logic of your order.

'Your essay sounds like someone working at a computer, following up different options to see where they lead you. The computer knows exactly where you're at, but your reader doesn't.'

Vicky said, 'Now I wonder why that should be?'

Task 2 (20 Minutes)
In about 50 words for each case, say what each student in the case studies learns about keeping to the purpose.

Summary

To produce an effective piece of continuous writing, you must:
- first identify the purpose;
- decide on the content;
- plan;
- collect information;
- draft;
- write and rewrite as necessary.

You can improve your essay writing techniques by:
- studying the techniques used in other kinds of writing;
- practicing those techniques;
- adapting them for essays.

Identify the specific requirements for your essay by:
- checking with your tutor;
- checking with the examination body.

36 *Little Red Book of Essay Writing*

Choosing Your Topic

The difficulties and disagreements are mainly due to the attempt to answer questions, without first discovering precisely what question it is you desire to answer.

To do yourself justice, try to choose the topics that will enable you to make the most of your knowledge and skills. First, remind yourself of the requirements of an essay.

Memory Check

Jot down the requirements of an essay – the proofs of your abilities that an essay might be expected to show.

Understanding The Title

'Marry in haste, repent at leisure' applies to choosing essay titles. Make sure you know what is wanted. First use common sense to grasp what the title as a whole expects.

My First Day at Secondary School

This has no instructional word, but you can take it to be 'tell the story of' or 'describe' or 'give your memories of'. Would you simply recount the main events in chronological order? No — you would describe your memories and feelings as vividly as possible; you would bring to life your fellow pupils and teachers, try to show why your memories are significant, and perhaps reflect on what they tell you about yourself.

Answer the question

The most common fault in essays is failure to answer the question— to do what the title requires. In exams this failure may be a result of nerves. Anxiety to complete the exam in

Little Red Book of Essay Writing **37**

time may mean the question is not given the calm consideration it needs. But the term essay can also go off the point unless the question is both analysed carefully and constantly referred to.

Example

Consider this topic:
Argue the case against the banning of corporal punishment of children

Students who are against corporal punishment are liable to answer the wrong question — to argue the case, in other words, against corporal punishment. The topic requires exactly the opposite! The double negative 'against/ banning' becomes 'for' corporal punishment.

Refute the arguments that are made in favour of capital punishment is a title that might similarly lead astray: the positive words 'in favour of' can blur the negative effect of 'refute'.

> *NOTE:* For neither of the above argument topics does it matter what your view is. You are not judged by your view, only by how well you **argue a particular case.**

Keeping your Title in View

Misunderstanding can be avoided by constant reference to the topic.

- Write the title as a heading to your work at every stage – notes, plan, first draft, final version.
- Put the topic title on a card and display it above or on your desk.
- Paraphrase it, and if you're not sure that you've got in right, check with your tutor or fellow students.

38 *Little Red Book of Essay Writing*

Paraphrasing the title

Example

Argue the case against the banning ofcorporal punishment of children could be paraphrased as:

'What are the arguments against making it illegal to give corporal punishment to children?'

Or

'What are the arguments for keeping it legal to give a reasonable amount of corporal punishment to children?'

An erroneous paraphrase would be:

'What are your views on whether or not corporal punishment of children should be made illegal?' It is not so much your views, as one side of the argument that must be focused on. *Worse would be:* 'What do you think about giving corporal punishment to children?' The crucial question of legality has disappeared.

In an exam, write the topic at the head of your essay: it is your title. Again, paraphrase it carefully if it could easily be misinterpreted.

Getting the question clear

When the topic is not expressed as a question, turn it into one. Here is another example:

'People don't seem to realise that it takes time and effort and preparation to think. Statesmen are too busy making speeches to think.

A suitable way of turning this into a question would be, 'How accurately do you think statement applies to the career of. .?

Then work out more questions to guide your reading, devoting a page or two of your notebook to them. Start question-making as soon as you can after receiving your assignment. Add questions that arise in the course of your reading.

Little Red Book of Essay Writing **39**

For example:
- What exactly do we mean by 'think'?
- How accurately does his statement apply to politicians generally?
- What were merits and defects as a thinker?

Memory Check

In about 12 to 15 words for each, write three examples of essay questions that might lead students astray if they didn't take care to analyse it.

Use for the *first:* 'Argue the case against ………….'

For the *second,* use: 'Refute the arguments that are made in favour of……'

Find your own formula for the *third.* Try them out on your colleagues to see if they fall into the trap.

Questioning the assumptions of the title

You might start to question assumption: Isn't the way a statesman thinks, you might argue, just as worthy of the name as the more sedentary, philosophical kind?

But common sense would bind you to the topic. You would still treat the quotation with respect and concentrate on applying it. Indicate clearly in the essay where you stand, and why. If totally at odds with the assumptions of a topic, you would be wise to choose another one.

Carry a notebook around. You may get ideas from anywhere — from radio, TV, conversations...

Understanding Key Terms And Instructions

We have been seeing the topics as a whole, considering what they are all about. Looking at the topics more closely you can see two or three different elements:

40 *Little Red Book of Essay Writing*

- **Key terms, or concepts.** These indicate what area of subject matter your essay should cover.
- **Instructional words.** These tell you what to do with the subject matter – explain it, compare/contrast it, discuss, argue a particular case or refute it, and so on.
- **Other pointers** to the meaning of the topic: for example, the many varieties of phrases that indicate your opinion is wanted: 'how far... to what extent...' and so on.

Interpreting key terms

Let us take these in order. What are they key terms in the punishment topic? They are:

- 'banning'
- 'corporal punishment'
- 'children.'

Banning has a clear enough meaning. Can there be doubt about what the other two terms mean? Well, yes, there can! Take corporal punishment: when does a nudge become a tap, a tap become a smack, a smack become a blow, a blow become an assault? If you are doing the essay

Table of Instructions

Instruction	What it means
analyse	discuss in detail, examine, criticize, review
appraise	evaluate, find the value of
assess	weigh up, judge
compare	find similarities and differences between
contrast	indicate the differences between
criticise	give your assessment of merits and defects

Little Red Book of Essay Writing **41**

define	give the precise meaning of
discuss	examine in detail, argue, give reasons for and against
describe	give a detailed account, discuss
examine	investigate, scrutinize, discuss
explain	account for, give reasons for, make clear
indicate	point out, show
illustrate	explain with examples
interpret	explain the meaning of
judge	give your opinion/conclusion
justify	give reasons for, show to be true or reasonable
outline	give main points, showing structure, omitting details
refute	prove a statement/argument to be false
relate	make the connections clear between facts and events
state	present simply and clearly
summarise	give a brief account of the main points
trace	show the development of, in clear stages

You have to decide exactly where corporal punishment begins — and also where it turns into physical abuse, because that is another question.

When you start thinking about this, you realise that the age of the child comes into it, too. So you have to define 'children'. Is the school-leaving age, around 16, for example, the upper limit? How much force, at different ages, constitutes 'corporal punishment'?

Who's doing it? The question is should the rules for corporal punishment be the same for parent and teacher — or different?

You can see that by analysing the terms of the topic in

42 *Little Red Book of Essay Writing*

some detail, you are well on the way to a good plan for the essay.

General and specific meanings of terms

Use a dictionary to help you define a concept, but do so with caution. Be careful to consider not only the context of the topic but the discipline.

'*Poverty*' may be a straightforward term in most topics. But in sociological essays, when talking about poverty you normally consider the different approaches of theorists, with their varying definitions: from those who tend to see it as caused by individuals' problems, to those (for example Marxists) who see it as the product of a political system.

In literature, you have to be on the alert for terms carrying their contemporary meaning when the current meaning is different. A quotation may contain words carrying an original meaning some distance from its present day meaning. Here are a few examples (original meanings on the right):

addiction	inclination
conscience	knowledge
illness	ruthlessness
verbatim	orally

It is useful to underline the key terms in a topic. For example:

Argue the case against the banning of corporal punishment of children.

Task (Complete is 15 minutes)

(a) Underline the key terms in the following topics. Indicate which is the instructional word supplying it if it isn't explicit.

(b) Paraphrase each topic.

Little Red Book of Essay Writing **43**

1. Wisdom is wasted on the old. How far do you agree with this statement?
2. What may be the effects of an increase in leisure time?
3. Examine the significance of Brutus's role in Shakespeare's Julius Caesar.
4. Does the increasing popularity of fringe religious groups indicate that secularization is a myth?

Note that words can vary considerably in meaning according to the context, so use a dictionary with care.

Case Studies

Meena has written an essay called *'Cars should be banned from city centres.'* Her tutor asks her to read out the first paragraph:

Conditions in the cities are getting steadily worse: The increasing amount of traffic on the road. Something has to be done to remove cars from the city centres. Cars tend to pollute the air, cause congestion in the city centres, and are not very safe for both pedestrians and people living in and around these centres. As a result of this life is almost always at a standstill during the rush hour.

Comment

Q. 'What did you mean by "not very safe"'?
Ans. 'I meant because of the pollution.'

1. That, isn't clear from the sentence, is it? And why not just say that pollution damages the health of city dwellers? That would include the drivers, and all the other people around.
2. Notice by the way, that "The increasing amount of traffic on the road" is not a complete sentence. You should have

44 *Little Red Book of Essay Writing*

talked first about the congestion and life being at a standstill. Then about the pollution which is made worse by the standstill. *Read the next paragraph:*

The government is doing very little about these problems. The introduction of double yellow lines, red routes, traffic police and towing away cars is doing very little to stop the heavy flow of cars into the cities. The government should introduce an effective road and rail system, whereby people will leave their cars at, home and use public transport...

> *NOTE:* You need to link up the argument more clearly. You haven't mentioned banning yet. Start with your viewpoint — complete or partial banning. Then indicate what your argument is going to be briefly. One, the chaos of the city centres. Two, the inadequate efforts to deal with it. . . central government and local government. Three, what you think should be done: what effects banning them from the centres would have.

Another Example

For a one-off certificate course in Science and Technology one has written an essay in response to the question *'How accurately does the label "New Electric Age" characterise changes in everyday life between 1870 and 2010?'* The first paragraph may run:

The label 'New Electric Age' is a generalisation about changes in everyday life between 1870 and 2010. It is used to describe an 'average' person's everyday life between 1870 and 2010 but it is meaningless without putting the sampling population and deviations from it into context. In other words, to assess the validity of the label we need to look at whose lives were being described and how they were

Little Red Book of Essay Writing **45**

affected. It is also worth looking into who thought up the label and into the assumption behind it that science and technology would inevitably and increasingly give people a better life.

The body of the essay described the different aspects of life affected, industrial and domestic. The essay ended:

This label was created by scientists, technologists and entrepreneurs to promote the use of electricity. The ideology behind this label was that electricity technology would bring mankind a better and brighter future.

NOTE: The conclusion doesn't follow from the good analysis.

Summary

To choose a topic wisely, make sure you understand the title. These are the chief stage in the process of choosing:

☞ Study the title closely and avoid answering the wrong question.
☞ Is the time at your disposal sufficient, and are the books documents and other sources, readily available?
☞ Paraphrase the title as an aid to understanding it.
☞ Check your paraphrase with fellow students and /or tutor.
☞ Underline and interpret the key terms: note what they mean in context.
☞ Identify the instructions, and other pointers to what is wanted.
☞ Decide how far you agree with the title's assumptions.

46 *Little Red Book of Essay Writing*

Collecting the Information You Need

'Knowledge is of two kinds. We *know a subject ourselves, or we know where we can find information* upon it.'
Dr Samuel Johnson.

Improving Your Research Skills

Try to master the chief research skills. These are:
- organizing your time;
- relating the research to the topic;
- knowing where to find out;
- knowing how to use a library and the internet;
- reading purposefully;
- organising notes.

1. Organising Your Time

Make sure you meet the tutor's deadline. A late essay may not be accepted. If it is accepted, there may be a deduction of marks. Give yourself a timetable, working back from the deadline. Indicate the dates when you will need to:
- start writing up the final version;
- start writing the first draft;
- start thinking about the topic purposefully and making an essay plan;
- do any interviewing and do the note-taking from printed sources; deciding on the priorities;
- make a preliminary survey of sources that the topic demands.

2. Relating Your Research to the Topic

The title of your essay must be constantly referred to while researching so that you collect the information you need —

Little Red Book of Essay Writing   **47**

a little more than you need, so that you can select the most relevant, but not so much that you are bogged down or slowed down.

Example

Let's take a title already paraphrased:

What may be the effect of an increase in leisure time?

This would divide into such questions as: what changes will there be to:

1. the way society is ordered?
2. its institutions?
3. the way people live and work?
4. the educational system?
5. the entertainment industries?

First discover what ideas you may have in your mind. List them under each question. You may want to stimulate your thinking by using some kind of brainstorming method.

3. Knowing where to Find Out

Library research

☞ This means using all kinds of printed sources: books, booklets, magazines, newspapers, pamphlets, publicity materials, and so on.

☞ You may have been given book lists by your tutor perhaps one for the course and additional lists for each essay topic. Consult your tutor if you need help in selecting.

☞ Books may also be suggested during tutorials. You may be expected to add to any reading lists provided for essay topics: in other words part of the test may be to show research skills. Look at the bibliographies listed under encyclopedia entries on your subject. Look at the bibliographies provided in the books on your reading list.

48 *Little Red Book of Essay Writing*

4. Knowing how to use a library

Use a fairly large reference library regularly and get to know the librarian. You may have quickly learned where the various reference books are and how to use microfiche catalogues and computerised databases. But when you find sources for a particular essay hard to find, a friendly librarian may save you much time.

5. Knowing how to use the internet

The internet is invaluable for developing ideas but don't overdo the surfing or you will lose focus. Be careful to separate fact from opinion and to assess the value of opinions.

When you're looking for evidence to back up an argument, judge it according to its source. Questions to ask include:

- Is the information dated?
- Is the authorship known? Is it reliable?
- Is there propaganda? Special pleading?

The URL (the web page address) gives a guide to the reliability of the source. Check other sources. Citing net sources that are little known to back up a point won't do. The temptation to copy material from the internet without acknowledgement is dicey.

6. Legwork

This means finding out by using your legs and eyes. Go there and see for yourself (an old people's home, a football match).

Live research
This means research by interviewing. The quickest way to get the latest information on a current social problem may

Little Red Book of Essay Writing **49**

be to research like a journalist. You could, for example, interview the director or press officer of a voluntary association (pressure group); armed with their literature, you will be guided to the most recent articles published on the subject.

Other 'experts' might be interviewed.

An essay on prisons, for example, might benefit from an interview with an official of TIHAR Jail, a jailor or an ex-prisoner.

You will probably have formulated your interview questions during your reading, so that they are informed questions, relevant to your topic: questions that the printed sources have not, as far as you can gather, answered fully or have not yet caught up with. Surveys and questionnaires need to be prepared carefully to produce valid results — a skill that is learned as part of sociology and related courses.

Broadcast media and film

Check through the listings sections in newspapers and magazines to see if there are any programmes relating to the subject of your current project. Videos can sometimes be obtained from organisations that arepublicising their activities.

Reading Purposefully and Taking Notes

A common formula for an effective reading method is **SQ3R**:

S is for Sample
Q is for Question
R is for Read
R is for Recall
R is for Review

50 *Little Red Book of Essay Writing*

Sampling a book

The *sampling or surveying whether a book is suitable* involves looking at the:
- title
- author
- date of publication
- blurb
- contents page
- main headings
- index
- illustrations
- preface or introduction.

Question

Study the book in more detail. You will probably read the first and last paragraph of each page. What are the author's aims and how far are they achieved? Question the author's methods and ask yourself if you agree with the author's conclusions.

Read

You are now ready to read the book in more detail. Nevertheless, you may want to do this in two stages: first skimming or scanning, second in depth.
- **Skimming** means quickly exploring the ground covered, noting how the book relates to your essay topic.
- **Scanning** means that you know exactly what you want. Your search for the sections dealing with your concerns and ignore the rest.
- **In depth** means reading the relevant sections as slowly as necessary to understand, questioning critically as you go.

Little Red Book of Essay Writing **51**

There are study guides that help you to check your reading efficiency and to read faster. You may want to prepare for note-taking as you read by putting notes in the margin of your own books, or on photocopied material, or by underlining or highlighting parts of the text.

It is best to read quickly through a text before note- taking, so that you see what is essential. Time can be wasted taking too many notes, and they can defeat the purpose of note-taking. Notes taken from a long text normally need to have page numbers or section headings indicated.

Recall

Recall and review are what you do when you meet a memory check in this book. You will improve your memory by regular recalls, at the end of each chapter or section. Recall orally or in writing.

1.Oral recall

For oral recall get a fellow student to ask you factual questions on the text. As each answer is approved, write it down.

2.Written recall

For immediate written recall, first write the marginal notes and do the underlining; study these preliminary notes. Then cover them and reproduce them, fleshing them out as necessary.

Review

Go back through the text quickly. Add to your notes anything important you have left out. At a later stage, just before an exam perhaps, or just before handing in an essay, you will

52 *Little Red Book of Essay Writing*

probably want to repeat this review, and you may then find one or two more gaps in your notes.

Memory Check

Close the book and explain the **SQ3R** reading method to your class or a fellow student, who will be following the text and will prompt you if necessary.

Practising Note-taking

Practise taking notes from different kinds of texts so that you develop your techniques. Using quality newspaper leaders is recommended: their subject-matter will be varied and styles will be varied. You will find in many a mix of narrative, description, exposition and argument. Choose clear, straightforward leaders. Before attempting the following task, study the sample of note-taking shown in Appendix B.

Task

Open a quality (broadsheet) daily newspaper at the leader page.

1. Skim-read the first leader, numbering each paragraph and giving it a heading.
2. Then read it in-depth, underlining the main points and listing them in the margin by placing (a), (b), (c) and so on alongside them.
3. Scan-read to fix the main points and the structure in your mind.
4. Close the newspaper and write down your notes of the leader in this schematic form.
5. Check with the leader to see if you have left out any important points.

Little Red Book of Essay Writing **53**

Deciding What and How to Note

Your course outline

For all disciplines you should make a course outline. You may have been given one by your tutor. Expand this into a larger framework so that when taking notes you will see where they fit into the course as a whole. Make notes on the jargons and on the formulae for different disciplines.

Making A Bibliography

Make a bibliography of all books and other printed sources consulted. It is useful to indicate briefly for each reference the value of the book for course and essay purposes; show what notes were taken, in case you may want to go back to the book later on.

Notes from books

Note chapter headings of books you may want to study more fully at a later stage. Use the indexes to guide you through a book where the information you need is scattered. Put page numbers or chapter section headings alongside notes taken in case you need to check later:

Always check quotes (what people have said) and quotations (literary references).

Different disciplines make different note-taking demands. Most require you to collect your own thoughts/reactions as you research. You may want to add, especially for long projects, your immediate reactions to details noted. Such details may include facts that you believe are false and will want to check, and opinions you believe are erroneous. Insert your own thoughts/reactions in square brackets so that they won't be confused with others' opinions. Or you may want to include suitably labelled notes for a future project.

54 *Little Red Book of Essay Writing*

For literature, history, politics and other subjects, a narrative summary may provide a convenient framework, with the important events, periods and stages given dates.

Notes from other sources

Whatever sources of information are used, it is easy to get it wrong. Practising note-taking in the way described above — always checking back with the original — will alert you to any careless reading, thinking and interpreting habits you may have developed. Take notes from newspapers and magazines with special care, and find time to check with at least one other source.

A newspaper report may be flawed in various ways: Lack of time and space means that the selected facts add up to an incomplete picture. Facts may be omitted through a reporter's prejudice, conscious or unconscious, or because of the paper's political leaning. A National Front organ may play down the racism in a particular area. Be on the alert for opinion presented as if it were news.

Study feature articles in newspapers and magazines with an eagle eye for factual errors and flaws in argument. Don't assume that books must have the facts correctly. If in doubt, express your doubt. Better still, check against another source.

Testing for reliability

Are the facts adequate to support the opinions expressed? Are the arguments convincing? Are they weakened by political bias or other kinds of faulty reasoning?

Take notes in your own words. Repeating chunks of other writers' work in an essay is very noticeable. It shows that you haven't formed your own ideas about the subject matter. Put quote marks around passages you want to quote as evidence. When taking notes from lectures and interviews,

Little Red Book of Essay Writing **55**

ignore ramblings and write down only the essential points. Practise with tape-recordings of talks, then play them back to see what you have missed.

The visual-minded may prefer to take notes in diagrammatic forms (mind maps).

Organising Your Notes

How elaborately you organise notes is a personal matter, but the following arrangements are recommended for university level if not before. Try them, and make short cuts where you feel you can.

1. Labelled folders containing various materials, including brochures, leaflets, newspaper cuttings and photocopied extracts. Once used for an essay, they should be kept for possible future projects.
2. Loose-leaf ring binders containing notes on A4 sheets. Write on one side of the paper only on A4 pads, double-spaced with margins to make any additions easier. You may need dividers to separate different aspects of a lengthy project.
3. 6" X 4" cards, easier to put in order by shuffling, particularly for assay.
4. 5" X 3" bibliography cards; can be finally shuffled into alphabetical order.
5. 5" X 3" cards for jargon and formulae.

Organising reference material

Facts, figures, research findings, opinions, ideas: if you have gathered these from your reading or web surfing (or perhaps by interviewing experts), then the source must be acknowledged (in other words, referenced). They must not be presented as if they came out of an infinite store of

56 *Little Red Book of Essay Writing*

knowledge inside your head! NOTE: statements given as facts in the media may be inaccurate and may need double checking.

Teachers/tutors/examination boards may have preferences for the way references are included in the body of your essay and listed below it. The rules are more extensive at tertiary level and students are generally given a style sheet to follow. A common requirement is for references to articles in newspapers, magazines and journals to be in single quotes and for book titles to be in italics as shown on the bibliography cards.

Case Studies

A student joins a research team

'A movement born out of conflict'; the history of the Trades Union Congress.
        Or
'To what extent has the power of the trade unions decreased since 1980?'

The student perhaps always reads the last paragraph of anything first, declared that the relevant points were well summed up in the last paragraph and he read it.

Another Topic:

'How effective are the media in their watchdog role?'

Comment

This is quite a long project, so it would be best to divide it up. Keep all notes on campaigns, for example, together, on one side of a page or pages. Or use cards. Then when you're ready to write, you can shuffle your notes in the order of your plan — or experiment with different orders.

Little Red Book of Essay Writing **57**

Wide margins and double spacing should be left for this purpose.

BEWARE: You've learnt that it can be unwise to borrow other students' lecture notes.

Try a for-and-against pattern

How far is it true to say that word-processors help you to write better?

AGAINST	FOR
(1) Just an instrument.	(2) Can correct quickly and move blocks of text around.
(2) Can make your feel it's better because mechanics are easier.	(4) Programs to check spelling and even grammar.
(5) Easier: can make you less fussy.	(6) Easier: you don't mind correcting many drafts.

NOTE: This is a repetitive pattern of each point suggesting it's opposite. Take another sheet of paper and re-write:

Just an instrument but only

but corrects quickly

but only feels better bec easier

but more time for the writing

but can make you less fussy

Now is the approach to the title was: 'help' means 'make it easier' (to write better), but balanced against this was the fact of inherent laziness. Some writers would use the extra time and energy to make it better, others would reduce their efforts. First we may continue with the thinking in 'buts'.

58 *Little Red Book of Essay Writing*

Then we would take each aspect (mechanics, speed, and so on) and set advantages against disadvantages in the same way.

We could support arguments with the many technical facts he knew about word-processors, but he would need to weigh in with other highly informed opinion. We would send a questionnaire round colleagues at work. For opinions without too much evidence behind them he would use words like 'may be' and 'theory', as tutor suggested. This is an essay that was firmly rooted in the real world — and his world at that!

Summary

The main research skills are:
☞ relating the research to the topic at all stages of the work;
☞ knowing how to use a library and the internet, knowing how to observe and how to interview;
☞ reading purposefully (using the formula SQ3R);
☞ note-taking and organising notes effectively.

Putting your Ideas into a Design

'Thinking means connecting things, and stops if they cannot be connected.' G K Chesterton,

Effective Thinking

1. For essays, *thinking* means connecting the knowledge you have amassed about the subject, shaped and adapted by your own thoughts and ideas, to the demands of the topic.

Little Red Book of Essay Writing   **59**

2. *Planning* means making your thinking effective: putting what you have to say in logical order, with clear connections between the parts so that you achieve unity and coherence.

In practice, you are thinking and planning simultaneously, but giving extra attention to the more creative approach — finding ideas — or to the more analytical approach — putting the ideas in order, when required. Try out the various suggestions in this chapter and discover what kind of switching back and forward between the two suits you best.

What are the hardest things about essay planning?

Thinking effectively is particularly difficult at certain points in the essay planning process. At which point do you find it hardest? Consider these emergency points:

1. At the start: when first confronted with the topic.
2. When switching gear, i.e. from gathering information to imposing order on it.
3. When the plan doesn't work—some connections are weak or lacking.
4. When you have digressed.
5. When a clear conclusion is slow to emerge.
6. When an introduction is elusive.
7. When blocked at any point in thinking, planning or writing.

Planning Tactics

There are various planning tactics that will help you to effective thinking. Some or all might be employed for one essay. Any of them might help at one of the emergency points. The tactics are:

- building on your controlling idea;
- brainstorming for ideas: the creative approach;

60 *Little Red Book of Essay Writing*

- putting your points in order: the analytical approach;
- finding the best pattern to develop;
- choosing the plan that fits the topic;
- sharpening your plan.

Building on your Controlling Idea

Your controlling idea is a summary of what you have to say in your essay in one sentence. You need a controlling idea round which the parts will gather to give your essay unity and coherence before you attempt a final plan. You can call that *controlling idea a thesis, a theme, an explanation, a considered view* — depending on the kind of essay.

You may have found a good controlling idea before making notes. It may have been immediately suggested by the essay title. On the other hand, your ideas might come thick and fast; and at the end of note-taking you may still be far from deciding on a controlling idea. You still don't know what you think, or you still don't see how to argue a particular case or explain some process. If so, don't plan too soon.

Write first, plan later
Tell yourself it's because you're creative. Write first, plan later.

☞ Read through your notes but don't be daunted if they are numerous. Either you eat your notes, or they eat you. Put them aside.

☞ Make false starts, tear up and start again. A plan, together with a controlling idea, will emerge. You can then go back to the notes to flesh it out.

With a topic such as: *'Is happiness the thing to aim at?'* — you may find it more productive to keep up a flow of several drafts, reshaping and refining your ideas as you go.

Little Red Book of Essay Writing **61**

You may prefer to write first, plan later, or keep drafting, whatever the topic.

Brainstorming for Ideas

This is particularly useful at the start of thinking, or of planning, or at the start of writing, or at any point where you get stuck or find your ideas too predictable. The techniques let you trigger your imagination, and produce fresh ideas. They can evoke patterns that will show you how to order your facts and ideas in interesting ways, whether you're working from notes or not.

- **Brainstorming** means experimenting with word and idea associations, particularly making unusual associations, to see what happens.

Example
Topic: *'Have the feminists gone too far?'*

Your immediate reaction might be 'I don't know'. Don't worry. The tutor is not expecting wisdom nor even balanced argument in these circumstances. What is hoped for is a point of view expressed persuasively (good practice towards argument). It can be entertaining, even humorous.

When you have paraphrased it : 'To what extent do you think that the campaigners for recognising the rights and increasing the opportunities of women have produced harm as well as benefits?'-you may find ideas beginning to arrive. But you can build further, with 'associations'.

Using the Five Ws of association

Associate your essay subject with words that relate to real life. An essay must provide evidence for points made. **Evidence means examples.** Examples can be found or created by associating your subject with:

62 *Little Red Book of Essay Writing*

☞ people   (who)
☞ places   (where)
☞ activities, events, situations   (what)
☞ times   (when)
☞ reasons   (why)

To this add processes (how). In brackets are the '**Five-Ws- plus-How**' questions that the newspaper reporter keeps mind to collect information for a report.

You might find these questions easier to use. How do they relate to your topic? You are now ready to write down how the evidence might be grouped:

Who	working class people, middle-class, housewives, people in different occupations/professions....
Where	at school, at home, at work, at leisure......
What	housework, family life, education, occupations...
When	times/occasions when feminist campaigners have delayed progress
Why	arguments such as 'it's man's world' or 'women deny their nature trying to be men' to explain why particular views of feminism are held
How	ways in which women/men are discriminated against.

Using people and perspectives

A slimline version of the above technique can be described as 'people and perspectives'. For example, you are faced with:

What was Anna Hazare's quarrel with Corruption?

Your interest may be firmly engaged in Indian politics but you can't see a path through all the facts (or you're sitting an exam and feel hopeless at remembering facts).

Furthermore, we'll say, you're young, and like most young students you tend to repeat the generalisations without fully grasping them.

Little Red Book of Essay Writing **63**

Example 1: People and perspectives means how do (or would) certain people, or groups of people, or professions, or institutions, react to (or within) your subject? Let's apply it to the current facts. You've already got the people. So the approach is: how did they react to corruption? Avoid the details of the constitutional argument? To do this, imagine yourself as the common man: what is your attitude to the Government? By moving back from the clouds of facts you are freer to think and to reveal your historical imagination. The significant facts you need for signposts are also more likely to present themselves when you are thinking in a fruitful way.

Example 2: Applying people and perspectives to *the feminism topic,* how do certain key groups of people (professions, for example) relate to feminism? How far have opportunities for women advanced within them? Teachers?Lawyers?Doctors?Actors?

Should there be more prisons or fewer?

Will it benefit — if it is not too obvious — from showing perspectives of ex-prisoners, social workers, police, victims of crime and priests as well as from (if it is sociology) the theories of the academics.

Using random associations

Brainstorming more freely may be worth trying if nothing of much interest or originality is emerging from your thinking and planning.

- **Random association** means putting alongside a concept –let's say 'punishment' words picked out at random from a planning.

  Here we go. Punishment and — dedication — euphemism — H-bomb — orphanage — cellotape — squib — triangle

64 *Little Red Book of Essay Writing*

— woman. Punishment and euphemism might be an interesting connection. H-bomb and orphanage also suggests atrain of thought.

Bringing humour into your thinking is one more way of escaping from the straitjacket of logic that can prevent you from seeing things in an original way. Edward de Bono's books on 'Lateral Thinking' describe many more liberating techniques.

Using mind maps

Write down your word and idea associations in **a pattern called a mind map** (also known as a *mind web, a 'spider'* or a *concept tree*).

You can develop the map into a logical plan if it needs more order, or work on it until it makes a comprehensive plan in itself. The mind map is particularly useful as a visual plan for an essay exam. It is also worth trying for note-taking, whether for essays or business reports.

'What are the causes of violence in cities?'

Setting out points one by one under the headings in the formal manner might be a safer way of being comprehensive. But the mind map makes you think of (and see at a glance when you've finished) the more surprising relationships, like seeing a landscape from the air.

Memory Check

Close the book, and in 60 words (20 for each) write explanations of the three **brainstorming techniques – 5 Ws,** people and perspectives, and random associations.

Little Red Book of Essay Writing **65**

Putting your Points in Sequence/order

When imposing order on given facts and opinions, rather than discovering ideas, is likely to be the emphasis, you will benefit most from formal plans. Base them on:

Introduction	beginning
Body	middle
Conclusion	end

Your planned introduction and conclusion may be provisional until you have finished writing.

On the other hand, if you have come to a definite conclusion at the planning stage, or at the start of writing, it will help you to avoid digressing.

Finding the Best Pattern to Develop

From your quick read-through of the notes or from the rough sketch of your ideas let a pattern or patterns emerge:

- Is it a narrative, requiring mainly a chronological order?
- Does the narrative need further ordering- some kind of historical exposition for example-origins, developments, effects?
- Will further subdivision be necessary: for example, political, social, economic?
- Should there be climax or anti-climax order-most important first or most important last?
- Is it an exposition/argument requiring an order of cause and effect?
- Will an exposition be done by definition, analysis, clarification (notably by clearing away misconceptions about the subject), comparison, explanation of relationships?

66 *Little Red Book of Essay Writing*

- Will an argument be developed by presentation of evidence, by analogy, by induction (from the particular to the general), by deduction (from the general to the particular), or from past experience (for example, you can expect certain trends in the economy because it is cyclical)?

The more essays you write, the more instinctively you will choose the right shape for the purpose. Here are some techniques of the formal kind.

Choosing a Plan to Fit the Topic

Building points into paragraphs

A straightforward essay needing little exposition or argument can be planned with a list of points. Five hundred words on:

A child's visit to the Museum

For example, might be ordered under:

1. Mummies.
2. Weapons.
3. Gold.
4. Jewellery.
5. Sculpture.
6. The Gift Shop.

☞ Give a paragraph to each point; 70 words for each paragraph (total 420 words)

☞ 50 words for an introductory

☞ 30 words for a concluding paragraph.

- *'What happens when you are arrested'* and *'How to cook curry'* would be equally easy to arrange.

Question-per-paragraph plan: The questions that it was suggested could be raised before, during and after planning

Little Red Book of Essay Writing **67**

could be put in order and used as a question-per-paragraph plan.

- *Should parents be responsible for the crimes of their children?*

Your questions might run something like this:

- Is the quality of parental guidance deteriorating?
- Is there insufficient discipline/motivation to learn in the schools?
- Are the resources of the police insufficient to cope with delinquents?
- Is the law inadequate and are the courts too busy to cope?
- Do the media (and particularly TV) set up too many unworthy role models?
- Do current standards of behaviour in society at large provide bad examples?

☞ At 500 words it would be an opinion piece.

☞ If you had 1,000 words, you would no doubt be expected to do some research. Your questions would be added to and improved. You might then give more than one paragraph to any issue that demanded more space.

Statement-per-paragraph plan

This is particularly suitable for a straight-through logical exposition/argument, and if you insert the links the writing-up will stay on the path. For example, an economics essay on *'The Costly Misconceptions about Risks'* might be planned like this:

1. Introduction. Examples of misconception: the car driver is 18 times more likely to die in a car crash than a train passenger.
2. Yet continual safety improvements to trains paid for by increases in fares.

68 *Little Red Book of Essay Writing*

3. This results in more people taking to roads-which are more dangerous.
4. These decisions are based on many public misconceptions about daily risks.
   (a) building regulations: the estimated cost is 23 million for each life saved;
   (b) Cancers are considered twice as frequent as heart diseases (but strokes are ten times more frequent).
   (c) Murders are considered to be as common as strokes (but strokes are ten times more frequent).
5. Conclusion: The blame for getting expenditure decisions wrong can be attributed to public mistrust of experts.

Producing a detailed outline

It's a good idea to note points for your introduction and conclusion.

Vetting Your Plan

Here is a checklist for vetting your plan:
- Is there a unified theme with a logical progression?
- Is every point necessary?
- Are they well connected?
- Does the introduction make it clear what the essay is all about, and what the viewpoint is?
- Do introduction and conclusion chime?
- Is the conclusion firmly backed up by the evidence of the body?

Task

☞ Study: 5 minutes
☞ Writing the plan: 20 minutes

Make a detailed outline of the same length for an essay on:

Little Red Book of Essay Writing **69**

Has the anti-smoking campaign gone too far?

Include brief Introduction and Conclusion sections as in the model. Come to a conclusion for or against, but put both sides of the argument. You may use the following points, which are out of order, for the body, and add to them;

1. Danger to health of others.
2. Government gains much revenue from sales of tobacco.
3. Anti-social behaviour: 'dirty habit', smell on clothes, breath, etc.
4. 'An addiction rather than a pleasure.'
5. Bad example to children.
6. Dangers to health : cancer etc.
7. Smoking is a basic human right.
8. 'A pleasure rather than an addiction.'
9. The cost to the taxpayer of keeping smokers alive/in health.

Summary

Planning is a way of making sure you think effectively, so that your essay has unity and coherence, with all the connections in the right places. Plans are of two kinds:

1. 'creative' or 'informal'
2. 'linear-logical', or 'formal.'

Creative plans are produced by such brainstorming experiments as the **Five Ws** association — asking **Five Ws-plus-How**. This can be simplified into the people and perspectives formula. The game of random associations is another technique.

70 *Little Red Book of Essay Writing*

Making your Essay Coherent

Carry the reader with you by keeping to the point and making clear connections.

You may find it easier to write your essay if you get the introduction right first — you then see how to proceed. Or you may prefer to get the conclusion right first — seeing the destination all the time keeps you on track.

But spending time on these parts is usually more fruitful when you see what you've said, when you've built the body. Building the body, therefore, is what the next two chapters will concentrate on.

The Three-part Structure

Unity and coherence: the three parts hang together:

Introduction

Indicate:
* What you understand by the title;
* What your objectives are;
* Which aspects of the subject your will deal with;
* What you will explain or argue.

The body

* Build up your explanation/argument with ideas, opinions and facts.
* Support key points by examples and other evidence, using your own thoughts and experience, and the statements of authorities.

Conclusion

* Sum up; return to the title, or echo it in some way.

Little Red Book of Essay Writing **71**

- Show that you have answered the question, or arrived at a point of view; possibly speculating on the future.

  You must try to know how to:
  - get in the mood to write;
  - start writing;
  - keep to the point.

Getting In The Mood To Write

☞ Essays can be competent but cold. You may have conceived yours with feeling. You may have fought hard to get it right, painstakingly searched for the right phrases, tinkered with the shape, only to find that the heat has dispersed, that the life and the soul have gone out of it.

☞ With a deadline, you may not have time to wait for the mood to rewrite. In any case, this may be the worst thing you could do. Instead, you can create the mood.

☞ When you start to write, make sure that you are full of interest in your subject, keen to communicate what you have to say. Much reading and thinking may have had a mind-numbing effect.

Getting warmed up

Three suggestions for loosening up and warming up (use one or more):

1. Talk to fellow students until your feeling re-emerges.
2. Skim through your notes to find a point, an argument, a telling image that excites you and gives you a starting point.
3. Read something near in subject-matter to your projected essay, but not too close — an article, perhaps, or a chapter of a book. Alternatively, a play, a film, or a TV programme may do the rekindling.

72 *Little Red Book of Essay Writing*

4. Your brain may need more oxygen. If so for a walk or jog! This will help!

These tactics can be tried out at any stage of writer's block.

Starting to Write

Six ways of starting to write: Use the combination that suits you.
- Talk yourself into it.
- Take a starting point, and plunge in.
- Re-start from warm.
- Correct as you go.
- Extend paragraph to essay.
- Use a mind map.

Talk yourself into it

☞ Select your audience
☞ Tell them (briefly) what you've found out about the subject
☞ See how they react.
☞ Do they understand what you're saying, or are you still far from getting your thoughts in order?
☞ The conversation will force you to get your thoughts in better order, and a controlling idea for your essay might emerge, if it hasn't already.

Ask them:
1. 'What would you want to know from this essay?'
2. 'What questions would you ask if you were doing it?'
3. 'What would be your key question?'
   You might get a provisional introduction out of them that will send you on your way. Something like:
   'Mention *capital punishment* in the course of conversation and you may be bombarded with many points of view:

Little Red Book of Essay Writing **73**

'Whatever views people hold on capital punishment, very few would disagree that...'

Take a starting point, and plunge in

It might be an anecdote, a joke, an image, a quote, a question. If its relevance hits you between the eyes, put it down, and keep writing. You have thrown a stone into a lake and you're watching the patterns made by the ripples.

You might decide to omit the first paragraph or two when you've come to the end, but it will have served its purpose.

Keep going. You don't have to be linear. Learn from the painter and the sculptor. Jump into the middle and build round it. A portrait painter won't labour for hours getting every detail of the eyes right before moving down.

Re-start from warm

When the writing takes several sessions, especially when there are days in between, make sure you don't have to restart from cold. Get into the next sentence or two of your essay, knowing how you will continue.

Correct as you go

Are you a corrector-as-you-go? That way may work better for you than concentrating on maintaining the flow of a draft, especially if you have a word processor. You may go through several drafting journeys in one continuous operation. But you could consider that certain essays which tend to be produced by going deeper into layers of thought, one after the other (philosophy, history, political theory) might suffer from being beaten up before they're strong enough to fight back.

74 *Little Red Book of Essay Writing*

Find better words and phrases as you go, but avoid making radical changes. Print out drafts and make major alterations on these. Keep previous drafts until you're sure of the end product. When a machine makes it so easy to delete and rearrange your sentences, at least give them some time to speak up for themselves.

Adapt brainstorming techniques for planning into techniques to get you writing. But first:

Memory Check

Write one sentence on each:
1. What is the 'people and perspectives' formula?
2. Explain the question-per-paragraph plan.
3. Explain the statement-per-paragraph plan.

Now here is a strategy for rapidly turning this kind of planning into a draft.

Extend paragraph to essay

Take, for example the topic:

Should parents be responsible for the crimesof their children?

☞ Reorder the questions more effectively, if you see a way.

☞ Replace any of the questions, if better ones occur to you.

☞ The advantage of putting them all into one paragraph first is that you begin to see them, not as separate points, but as points that together make a whole.

☞ The unity of that original paragraph will be reflected in your finished essay.

Now, in this original paragraph, after each question you could put a statement — a rough guide to the kind of answer you might develop — or another question. Underline a link or two if they come to mind, or wait until they come to mind in the course of writing up.

Little Red Book of Essay Writing **75**

Example
You might begin:

Is the quality of parental guidance deteriorating? There seems little doubt that a general weakening of religious and moral convictions makes parents less confident about guiding their offspring. Is there a similar cause for the lack of discipline and of motivation to learn reported in many schools..?

You could then use your notes for these additional statements or questions, or you could develop your thoughts as you go.

You are now ready to begin the essay proper. Each pair of sentences (question plus statement or two questions) makes the beginning of each paragraph of your essay. Fill out each paragraph as you go. Swoop into your notes when you feel the need, but if you have a lot of notes avoid slowing yourself down into a writer's block.

Use a mind map

Let us see how the mind map on page 63 could quickly get you writing. After studying this for a minute or so, you could number and label five sectors:

What are the causes of violence in inner cities?

1. Violence defined — kinds of violence and where directed.
2. Various general causes.
3. How tensions build up — explode — children learn violent ways.
4. Crimes of violence — how they follow attempts to escape from causes/effects of poverty (alcohol, drugs).
5. Violence breeding violence — for example, in the slums.

76 *Little Red Book of Essay Writing*

Keeping to The Point

☞ *An essay must keep to the point.*

☞ Be as simple and direct as the subject and the purpose allow.

☞ Your essay must have unity and coherence.

☞ The parts should be in orderly, logical sequence adding up to one theme

☞ They should be clearly linked.

☞ MOST IMPORTANT: keep the title in front of you as you write.

Try to carry the reader along in the flow, as the experienced driver carries a passenger in a car. Confident in your ability, the reader should see clearly where the vehicle is going. A different destination may have been preferred, but there should be no complaints about the route to the destination that was chosen.

Using a network of connectives

The main techniques that achieve unity and coherence involve using connectives.

Types of connectives to use

Key words and ideas repeated

These will include the echoes of synonyms and near-synonyms. In the paragraph-essay on violence there are:

violence	escape
destroy	crime
consuming	vicious
fight	vicious
explode	spiral

Pronouns, demonstratives, definite article and comparative words: These refer to statements already made.

Little Red Book of Essay Writing   **77**

Examples are: he, she, it, we, this, that, these, those, the, equal, similar, such, bigger, the former, the latter.

Repeated grammatical patterns

Violence: 'There is the violence. . .there is the violence..., it can. . . it can...' (Use in moderation).

Signposting

You say, in effect, the foregoing has covered that; what follows will cover this. For example: *'Not only do visitors find the towns more lively than they had imagined, but the climate is also a pleasant surprise.'*

Miscellaneous links

Addition:	and, furthermore, moreover, what is more.
Contrast:	but, however, nevertheless, on the other hand, if the truth be told, admittedly, granted, it's true that.
Consequence:	so, therefore, the result was that.... hence, consequently, as a result..
Example:	for example, for instance, to put this more clearly.

Don't over-use these common links, however, just because they are readily available. The weather forecasters have constantly to guard against their 'buts'. Otherwise you will hear: 'It is a sunshine and showers day. This morning it will be mainly sunny, dry periods with some cloud... But showers will spread. . . But by late evening...'

Use the longer linking phrases sometimes when you are changing gear. This will prepare the reader smoothly and give breathing space: the reader uses the space to let the thoughts you've aroused so far settle into the necessary pattern. Use the rather more unusual links if they fit:

78 *Little Red Book of Essay Writing*

'Whether this way of putting it is wholly acceptable is a matter for debate...' is the sort of thing. Take them out of the second draft if they sound verbose.

TASK (15 minutes)

Project on smoking based on a questionnaire:

☞ Rewrite, improving the order and the links, and more concisely.
☞ Reduce by about a half. Include only the points made.

Project on Smoking

☞ Smoking include social reasons
☞ Some people enjoy it
☞ Pressure from their work and other stresses.
☞ Another reason given is pure habit, for example after each meal, any time they have to wait for something, or have a difficult job to do or after doing a difficult job, to relax.
☞ Other people say it stimulates them or makes them feel more cheerful in themselves.
☞ The social reasons are, when people smoke they do it in front of their friends who also smoke, this is socializing. Not surprisingly, smoking at the pub with friends who also smoke was the most popular reason. But nowadays the attitudes have changed, now it is drinking, while smoking is now a pest to society and people consider it as being anti-social. When people say they enjoy it I cannot comment because I am a non-smoker, but many people, when they try their first cigarette say 'Horrible!'

Little Red Book of Essay Writing **79**

Summary

Getting started

1. In the mood for writing means feeling keen to communicate, your ideas ready to flow. Talking, reading, exposing yourself to the subject or exercise may help to get you in the mood.
2. Starting and re-starting an essay can also be helped on by conversation. If an obviously suitable start doesn't quickly present itself, choose any possible way in: an image or a quote, for example.
3. Once the essay is launched, its momentum can be kept. up by various strategies. Choose the strategy that suits the kind of essay, and your temperament. You may prefer to correct as you go, or to maintain the flow by completing drafts before correcting.
4. Brainstorming techniques for getting started include extending summary-paragraph to essay, and using a mind map.

Keeping to the point

1. Keeping to the point means being as simple and direct as possible, with one controlling idea and with parts logically connected.
2. Connectives must be used skilfully so that you ensure clarity and coherence.
3. A well-structured essay is achieved by language skills, but it may lack life unless your interest in the subject has been so awakened that you have a strong desire to communicate it.

80 *Little Red Book of Essay Writing*

Giving Your Work Conviction

'True ease in writing comes from art, not chance.
As those move easiest who have learned to dance'
Alexander Pope (1688—1744)
Here are some effective ways to:
- narrate a story or piece of history;
- describe a scene or a process;
- analyse and explain a situation, process or procedure;
- argue a case and present it persuasively;
- fit a pattern to your subject;
- slot in your evidence;
- use anecdotes, quotes and quotations.

Each skill demands its own patterns.

☞ A combination of two or more patterns is usually required in an essay.

☞ Argument has to follow some analysis of the topic — division into its different aspects — and some exposition — explanation of the ways different viewpoints are arrived at.

☞ Analysis often follows description, particularly the special kind of description that is the defining of key terms.

☞ Narration — putting facts and events in an appropriate order — is rarely separate from description or from exposition. History is 'expository narration'. For convenience we shall discuss each skill separately.

How to Narrate

The narrative patterns in essays (following such instructional terms as 'relate', 'state' and 'trace') are clear and straightforward; they are not slowed down by unnecessary description. Chronological patterns are common but may be cut across by exposition patterns. For example, the extent of damage done by riots (effects) may need to be dealt with before causes.

A clear path to a climax

Climax order is often preferred to anti-climax because it is more readable: it avoids tailing off. The story-teller wants you to keep asking 'What happened next?' You can sometimes use the tricks of the story-teller in an essay. But if leaving the most important points (problems, solutions) till last produces suspense bordering on confusion, then you should sacrifice readability to clarity. In an essay you cannot afford to make the experiments that feature writers make in magazine articles, for example using a fictional technique like creating suspense to increase the drama of a situation.

How to Describe

As an essay topic instruction, describe means, as already noted, 'give a detailed account', discuss, as well as what it normally means. For example:

Describe the administration of your school
Or
Describe the functions and procedures of the Parliamentary Committees of Inquiry.

Being systematic

When describing, choose carefully the order of details. You need to give the reader a picture of the object or a clear pattern of the process. Chronological order may be involved. You may need to record the way something changes in the course of time (classrooms becoming more technological;

82 *Little Red Book of Essay Writing*

a landscape seen from a moving train). A town may need space order ('to the north. . .to the south. . . in the middle. . . round this. . . in the outskirts. . . ').

Making a word picture

To describe well in the more usual meaning of the term — to draw or paint an object, place, scene or person so that the reader sees it (smells it, and so on) — requires imagination and observational powers. These come through in vivid imagery and style with some originality. Such description is aimed at in creative essays and in incidental parts of others.

Nouns and verbs are as important as adjectives and adverbs. The latter must be chosen carefully so that your essay is not slowed down.

How to Analyse and Explain

Most essays are analytical in part, many are largely so. Get to know the different patterns expected by the various instructions you will meet. The following are quick, rough guides. Consider how they can be adapted to particular essay topics:

Analyse:	Break up into its parts or aspects or periods. Examine the merits and defects, or successes and failures.
Define and clarify:	Say exactly what it is. Correct misconceptions. Say what it isn't
Compare:	Say in what ways things are similar. Explain an unfamiliar object or idea by saying how it compares with an object or idea that is familiar.

Do you want your reader to remember your abstract explanations or arguments? Then provide examples —

Little Red Book of Essay Writing **83**

illustrations, anecdotes and analogies, or extended comparisons. In other words, translate abstract into concrete so that the reader can picture it. For example, you illustrate a famine with figures of people starving set against the amount of food available. An anecdote about Napoleon can give an insight into his character or achievement. You may want to explain how the brain works by using the analogy of a sophisticated machine.

Contrast: Explain how things actually differ that have similarities.

Assess: Give the pluses and minuses; sum up on the value.

Explain: Give causes of or reasons for.
Show how it has become what it is.
Show why it behaves as it does.

Be complete

Your exposition has to be knowledgeable so that the reader is prepared to believe what you say. It must also be complete, for if a gap is noticed, your credibility will suffer.

Using creative exposition

Instructions will sometimes demand some creativity in the way you approach the topic, but this is not always obvious.

Empathy assignments have as their aim 'to show an understanding of the points of view held by people in the past and to explain why they held them'.

The kind of information you are specifically looking for here is opinions, rather than character traits. A literary topic sometimes wants you to imagine yourself inside the author's or fictional character's head to reproduce the author's kind of creativity. (This is especially so if the novel is

84 *Little Red Book of Essay Writing*

psychological, and the reader is put into the protagonist's head from the word go. The kind of imagination sometimes wanted by a history topic, in contrast, is your historical imagination. Can you relate those opinions, feelings, reactions to historical facts? Of course the two kinds of imagination have much, more in common, but it is important to get the emphasis right, to harness the imagination to the discipline.

How to argue

What arguing means

To argue means to maintain by reasoning, to prove, to persuade. Before you argue, you generally have to clear the ground by some analysis, especially by:

- defining terms;
- clarifying issues;
- removing misconceptions.

Note that it is usually reasonable to set a limit when defining what most people would mean by a 'term' — you might decide that 'adults' in your essay means anyone who has finished school education; 'tragedy' in a literature essay might require a classical or a modern definition.

Inducing and deducing

There are *two main kinds of reasoning:*

Induction

Deduction

Induction

Induction means arguing from the particular to the general. For example, you suggest that because Delhi's citizens are increasingly worried about pollution of the atmosphere, and

Deduction means arguing from the general to the particular. As long as the general rule that you are basing your deduction on is well proven, the deduction is certain. For example: all cities contain a fair number of criminals. Delhi is a city. Therefore Delhi contains a fair number of criminals.

because Delhi is an average city, then the citizens of India's other cities will feel the same. The argument will only be as valid as your evidence. If Delhi, in fact, is likely to suffer much more from pollution than other cities, your argument tends to collapse.

Deduction
Deduction means arguing from the general to the particular. As long as the general rule that you are basing your deduction on is well proven, the deduction is certain. For example: all cities contain a fair number of criminals. Delhi is a city. Therefore Delhi contains a fair number of criminals.

Beware of fallacies!

A deduction such as this, in three parts, is called a **syllogism**:
- ☞ major premise
- ☞ minor premise
- ☞ conclusion

A **fallacy** — a flawed or misleading argument — occurs when your major premise is false. For example: all Indians are smart; Rakesh Sharma is an Indian; therefore Rakesh Sharma is smart. The reasoning process is valid, but the initial assumption is wrong.

A **fallacy** also occurs when the middle term doesn't follow the rules of logic, so that the conclusion doesn't necessarily follow. As in: Mentally ill people behave irrationally. Jeetender behaves irrationally. Therefore Jeetender is mentally ill. 'Behaving irrationally' in the minor premise does not have the same meaning as it does in the major premise. Call these false syllogisms.

Reasoning clearly
Practise thinking clearly when in discussions with friends:

86 *Little Red Book of Essay Writing*

- What exactly do you mean by that term?
- What is the evidence for that statement?
- Aren't you offering an opinion as if it were a fact?
- Is the argument valid but the assumption wrong?
- Is it a case of bias — 'you would say that, wouldn't you?'

But show your even-handedness by subjecting your own arguments to the same scrutiny. To maintain by reasoning means to produce convincing evidence, in the form of facts and informed (expert) opinions, to back up your beliefs.

The place for emotion in argument

To argue you need to be able to:
- reason well (think clearly);
- weigh evidence coolly;
- come to well-considered conclusions.

But the aim is to persuade, and emotion has its place in making the reader receptive to your reasoning. An essay on the homeless or on drug addiction will benefit from some attempt to get the reader sympathetic to the plight of the sufferers, especially at the start, to grab attention. Talking about literature is unthinkable without feeling.

In essays in the *'-ologies'*, on the other hand, emotion may be out of place — directly exploited, emotion certainly is. When aiming to be as objective as possible, you should be aware of exactly how emotion is operating in anything you write.

Your head must rule your heart in any essay, otherwise there will be serious flaws in your argument. Since flaws in an argument tend to be unconscious, show your work to your sharpest critic. Give that critic room in your head when you write. There are various kinds of flaws in argument and explains how to detect them.

Fitting A Pattern to your Subject

Different patterns, we have seen, cut across each other. For example, 'What were the causes of the First World War?' would have its chronological patterns broken into separate aspects — political, economic, and so on.

Essays on literature often require careful consideration of patterns. 'Trace the changes in Tagore's art by comparing and contrasting early, middle and late periods' suggests chronological order.

But many variations would be possible. For example:

- You could keep to the chronological basis suggested by the title. You could divide the essay into three main sections: early, middle and late. You could take one or two representative texts in each period, analysing each under such aspects as theme, plot, characterisation, language. You would note the changes in the author's art as you went, and sum up with your conclusions at the end.
- You could build each section round an aspect rather than round the period: four main sections rather than three. Thus you would trace the changes in the way Tagore dealt with themes right through the representative texts of each period, then plot, then characterisation, then language.
- You would decide how to slot into these patterns your viewpoint (or thesis), the objections (or antithesis), and your considered conclusion (or synthesis). In other words, you might draw together the main arguments at the end of each section, or leave the synthesis largely to the end of the essay.

Building to a climax

The main patterns of argument have been covered under exposition. Note that climax order, with its variations, is

88 *Little Red Book of Essay Writing*

generally more satisfying; it is more likely to hold the reader's interest than anti-climax. It has been pointed out that climax — with the sense of keeping the important till last — is not often suitable for down-to-earth, straightforward reports and investigations. But these will often use the variations of climax: for example, moving from the simple to the complex, or moving from the familiar to the unfamiliar.

Slotting In your Evidence

In both exposition and argument, you need to produce your evidence for your statements. This evidence has to be smoothly written in, otherwise your line of development will be blurred. Slot the references (exact quotes or quotations, or particular statements/opinions) into your plan: author, title, page number will suffice.

Example
A section of a plan for an essay in psychology reads:
Variations between scientific and commonsense approaches.
Some areas of study, less scientific, eg Freud.Pure scientific method, eg Skinner.
More flexible approach, eg Piaget.
There is sufficient linkage in the words, 'less', 'pure', and 'more' to suggest how to write it up.

Using Anecdotes, Quotes and Quotations

Used well, these elements can give an essay a lift.

Anecdotes

These are short, true stories, which are interesting or striking, and may be funny. They are a lively way of illustrating a point. They bring real life people into an otherwise abstract

Little Red Book of Essay Writing **89**

discussion. An anecdote about a parliamentary candidate being interviewed in his or her constituency, for example, may be a good way of revealing aspects of the interview procedure.

Quotes

Here we mean the exact words of someone interviewed — whether by yourself or an author; or extracts from published material.

Quotations

These are the well-known brief extracts from the statements of the famous, and for well-known extracts from literature. The first kind can be used to inject some humour, wit, or vivid image into an essay.

Quotations from literature, as used for discussion points for some of the chapters of this book, can quickly add resonance or an extra dimension to- your thoughts. But avoid, again, the too well known.

Both quotes and quotations must be used to support your points and must be directly relevant to the topic, not used for their own sake.

Using quotes as evidence

In literature essays your quotes (from published commentaries) and quotations (from studied texts) are key parts of the evidence for your interpretation or argument. Essays in psychology and sociology and others, which need to 'compare and contrast' the work of several authorities, may have to be content with brief statements of their positions rather than quotes. You may be expected to give title and page number for reference. Quotes from newspaper articles can be effective when dealing with current affairs.

90 *Little Red Book of Essay Writing*

Key Points

An essay can have many purposes, but the basic structure is the same no matter what. You may be writing an essay to argue for a particular point of view or to explain the steps necessary to complete a task.

Either way, your essay will have the same basic format.
If you follow a few simple steps, you will find that the essay almost writes itself. You will be responsible only for supplying ideas, which are the important part of the essay anyway.

Don't let the thought of putting pen to paper daunt you.

An essay can have many purposes, but the basic structure is the same no matter what. You may be writing an essay to argue for a particular point of view or to explain the steps necessary to complete a task.

Either way, your essay will have the same basic format.
If you follow a few simple steps, you will find that the essay almost writes itself. You will be responsible only for supplying ideas, which are the important part of the essay anyway.

Use this Sample Basic Essay as a Model

The essay below demonstrates the principles of writing a basic essay. The different parts of the essay have been labelled. The thesis statement is in bold, the topic sentences are in italics, and each main point is underlined. When you write your own essay, of course, you will not need to mark these parts of the essay unless your teacher has asked you to do so. They are marked here just so that you can more easily identify them.

Little Red Book of Essay Writing **91**

"A dog is man's best friend." That common saying may contain some truth, but dogs are not the only animal friend whose companionship people enjoy. For many people, a cat is their best friend.

Despite what dog lovers may believe, cats make excellent housepets as they are good companions, they are civilized members of the household, and they are easy to care for.

In the first place, people enjoy the companionship of cats. <u>Many cats are affectionate.</u> They will snuggle up and ask to be petted, or scratched under the chin. Who can resist a purring cat? <u>If they're not feeling affectionate, cats are generally quite playful.</u> They love to chase balls and feathers, or just about anything dangling from a string. They especially enjoy playing when their owners are participating in the game. <u>Contrary to popular opinion, cats can be trained.</u> Using rewards and punishments, just like with a dog, a cat can be trained to avoid unwanted behaviour or perform tricks. Cats will even fetch!

In the second place, cats are civilized members of the household. <u>Unlike dogs, cats do not bark or make other loud noises.</u> Most cats don't even meow very often. They generally lead a quiet existence. <u>Cats also don't often have "accidents."</u> Mother cats train their kittens to use the litter box, and most cats will use it without fail from that time on. Even stray cats usually understand the concept when shown the box and will use it regularly. <u>Cats do have claws, and owners must make provision for this.</u> A tall scratching post in a favorite cat area of the house will often keep the cat content to leave the furniture alone. As a last resort, of course, cats can be declawed.

Lastly, one of the most attractive features of cats as housepets is their ease of care. <u>Cats do not have to be</u>

92 *Little Red Book of Essay Writing*

<u>walked.</u> They get plenty of exercise in the house as they play, and they do their business in the litter box. Cleaning a litter box is a quick, painless procedure. <u>Cats also take care of their own grooming.</u> Bathing a cat is almost never necessary because under ordinary circumstances cats clean themselves. Cats are more particular about personal cleanliness than people are. <u>In addition, cats can be left home alone for a few hours without fear.</u> Unlike some pets, most cats will not destroy the furnishings when left alone. They are content to go about their usual activities until their owners return.

Cats are low maintenance, civilized companions. People who have small living quarters or less time for pet care should appreciate these characteristics of cats. However, many people who have plenty of space and time still opt to have a cat because they love the cat personality. In many ways, cats are the ideal housepet.

Topic Has Been Assigned

You may have no choice as to your topic. If this is the case, you still may not be ready to jump to the next step.

Think about the type of paper you are expected to produce. Should it be a general overview, or a specific analysis of the topic? If it should be an overview, then you are probably ready to move to the next step. If it should be a specific analysis, make sure your topic is fairly specific. If it is too general, you must choose a narrower subtopic to discuss.

For example, the topic "KENYA" is a general one. If your objective is to write an overview, this topic is suitable. If your objective is to write a specific analysis, this topic is too general. You must narrow it to something like "Politics in Kenya" or "Kenya's Culture."

Little Red Book of Essay Writing **93**

Once you have determined that your topic will be suitable, you can move on.

Topic has not been Assigned

If you have not been assigned a topic, then the whole world lies before you. Sometimes that seems to make the task of starting even more intimidating. Actually, this means that you are free to choose a topic of interest to you, which will often make your essay a stronger one.

Define Your Purpose

The first thing you must do is think about the purpose of the essay you must write. Is your purpose to persuade people to believe as you do, to explain to people how to complete a particular task, to educate people about some person, place, thing or idea, or something else entirely? Whatever topic you choose must fit that purpose.

Brainstorm Subjects of Interest

Once you have determined the purpose of your essay, write down some subjects that interest you. No matter what the purpose of your essay is, an endless number of topics will be suitable.

If you have trouble thinking of subjects, start by looking around you. Is there anything in your surroundings that interests you? Think about your life. What occupies most of your time? That might make for a good topic. Don't evaluate the subjects yet; just write down anything that springs to mind.

Evaluate Each Potential Topic

If you can think of at least a few topics that would be

94 *Little Red Book of Essay Writing*

appropriate, you must simply consider each one individually. Think about how you feel about that topic. If you must educate, be sure it is a subject about which you are particularly well-informed. If you must persuade, be sure it is a subject about which you are at least moderately passionate. Of course, the most important factor in choosing a topic is the number of ideas you have about that topic.

Even if none of the subjects you thought of seem particularly appealing, try just choosing one to work with. It may turn out to be a better topic than you at first thought.

Before you are ready to move on in the essay-writing process, look one more time at the topic you have selected. Think about the type of paper you are expected to produce. Should it be a general overview, or a specific analysis of the topic? If it should be an overview, then you are probably ready to move to the next step. If it should be a specific analysis, make sure your topic is fairly specific. If it is too general, you must choose a narrower subtopic to discuss.

For example, the topic "KENYA" is a general one. If your objective is to write an overview, this topic is suitable. If your objective is to write a specific analysis, this topic is too general. You must narrow it to something like "Politics in Kenya" or "Kenya's Culture."

Once you have determined that your topic will be suitable, you can move on.

Organise Your Ideas

The purpose of an outline or diagram is to put your ideas about the topic on paper, in a moderately organized format. The structure you create here may still change before the essay is complete, so don't agonize over this.

Decide whether you prefer the cut-and-dried structure of an outline or a more flowing structure. If you start one or the other and decide it isn't working for you, you can always switch later.

Diagram

1. Begin your diagram with a circle or a horizontal line or whatever shape you prefer in the middle of the page.
2. Inside the shape or on the line, write your topic.
3. From your centre shape or line, draw three or four lines out into the page. Be sure to spread them out.
4. At the end of each of these lines, draw another circle or horizontal line or whatever you drew in the centre of the page.
5. In each shape or on each line, write the main ideas that you have about your topic, or the main points that you want to make.
   - If you are trying to persuade, you want to write your best arguments.
   - If you are trying to explain a process, you want to write the steps that should be followed. You will probably need to group these into categories. If you have trouble grouping the steps into categories, try using Beginning, Middle, and End.
   - If you are trying to inform, you want to write the major categories into which your information can be divided.
6. From each of your main ideas, draw three or four lines out into the page.
7. At the end of each of these lines, draw another circle or horizontal line or whatever you drew in the center of the page.
8. In each shape or on each line, write the facts or information that support that main idea.

96 *Little Red Book of Essay Writing*

When you have finished, you have the basic structure for your essay and are ready to continue

Outline

1. Begin your outline by writing your topic at the top of the page.
2. Next, write the Roman numerals I, II, and III, spread apart down the left side of the page.
3. Next to each Roman numeral, write the main ideas that you have about your topic, or the main points that you want to make.
   - If you are trying to persuade, you want to write your best arguments.
   - If you are trying to explain a process, you want to write the steps that should be followed. You will probably need to group these into categories. If you have trouble grouping the steps into categories, try using Beginning, Middle, and End.
   - If you are trying to inform, you want to write the major categories into which your information can be divided.
4. Under each Roman numeral, write A, B, and C down the left side of the page.
5. Next to each letter, write the facts or information that support that main idea.

When you have finished, you have the basic structure for your essay and are ready to continue.

Compose a Thesis Statement

Now that you have decided, at least tentatively, what information you plan to present in your essay, you are ready to write your thesis statement.

Little Red Book of Essay Writing   **97**

The thesis statement tells the reader what the essay will be about, and what point you, the author, will be making. You know what the essay will be about. That was your topic. Now you must look at your outline or diagram and decide what point you will be making. What do the main ideas and supporting ideas that you listed say about your topic?

Your thesis statement will have two parts.

☞ The first part states the topic.
- ◆ Kenya's Culture
- ◆ Building a Model Train Set
- ◆ Public Transportation

☞ The second part states the point of the essay.
- ◆ has a rich and varied history
- ◆ takes time and patience
- ◆ can solve some of our city's most persistent and pressing problems

☞ Or in the second part you could simply list the three main ideas you will discuss.
- ◆ has a long history, blends traditions from several other cultures, and provides a rich heritage.
- ◆ requires an investment in time, patience, and materials.
- ◆ helps with traffic congestion, resource management, and the city budget.

Once you have formulated a thesis statement that fits this pattern and with which you are comfortable, you are ready to continue.

Write the Body Paragraphs

In the body of the essay, all the preparation up to this point comes to fruition. The topic you have chosen must now be explained, described, or argued.

98 *Little Red Book of Essay Writing*

Each main idea that you wrote down in your diagram or outline will become one of the body paragraphs. If you had three or four main ideas, you will have three or four body paragraphs.

Each body paragraph will have the same basic structure.

1. Start by writing down one of your main ideas, in sentence form. If your main idea is "reduces freeway congestion," you might say this: Public transportation reduces freeway congestion.

2. Next, write down each of your supporting points for that main idea, but leave four or five lines in between each point.

3. In the space under each point, write down some elaboration for that point. *Elaboration* can be further description or explanation or discussion.

Supporting Point
Commuters appreciate the cost savings of taking public transportation rather than driving.

Elaboration
Less driving time means less maintenance expense, such as oil changes.

Of course, less driving time means savings on gasoline as well.

In many cases, these savings amount to more than the cost of riding public transportation.

4. If you wish, include a summary sentence for each paragraph. This is not generally needed, however, and such sentences have a tendency to sound stilted, so be cautious about using them.

Once you have fleshed out each of your body paragraphs, one for each main point, you are ready to continue.

Little Red Book of Essay Writing **99**

Write the Introduction and Conclusion

Your essay lacks only two paragraphs now: the introduction and the conclusion. These paragraphs will give the reader a point of entry to and a point of exit from your essay.

Introduction

The introduction should be designed to attract the reader's attention and give her an idea of the essay's focus.

1. Begin with an attention grabber.

    The attention grabber you use is up to you, but here are some ideas:

    ◆ **Startling information**

    This information must be true and verifiable, and it doesn't need to be totally new to your readers. It could simply be a pertinent fact that explicitly illustrates the point you wish to make

    If you use a piece of startling information, follow it with a sentence or two of *elaboration*.

    ◆ **Anecdote**

    An *anecdote* is a story that illustrates a point.

    Be sure your anecdote is short, to the point, and relevant to your topic. This can be a very effective opener for your essay, but use it carefully.

    ◆ **Dialogue**

    An appropriate dialogue does not have to identify the speakers, but the reader must understand the point you are trying to convey. Use only two or three exchanges between speakers to make your point. Follow dialogue with a sentence or two of *elaboration*.

100   *Little Red Book of Essay Writing*

- ♦ **Summary Information**
  A few sentences explaining your topic in general terms can lead the reader gently to your thesis. Each sentence should become gradually more specific, until you reach your thesis.
2. If the attention grabber was only a sentence or two, add one or two more sentences that will lead the reader from your opening to your thesis statement.
3. Finish the paragraph with your thesis statement.

Conclusion

The conclusion brings closure to the reader, summing up your points or providing a final perspective on your topic.

All the conclusion needs is three or four strong sentences which do not need to follow any set formula. Simply review the main points (being careful not to restate them exactly) or briefly describe your feelings about the topic. Even an *anecdote* can end your essay in a useful way.

Add the Finishing Touches

You have now completed all of the paragraphs of your essay. Before you can consider this a finished product, however, you must give some thought to the formatting of your paper.

Check the order of your paragraphs.

Look at your paragraphs. Which one is the strongest? You might want to start with the strongest paragraph, end with the second strongest, and put the weakest in the middle. Whatever order you decide on, be sure it makes sense. If your paper is describing a process, you will probably need to stick to the order in which the steps must be completed.

Little Red Book of Essay Writing **101**

Check the instructions for the assignment.
When you prepare a final draft, you must be sure to follow all of the instructions you have been given.

- Are your margins correct?
- Have you titled it as directed?
- What other information (name, date, etc.) must you include?
- Did you double-space your lines?

Check your writing.
Nothing can substitute for revision of your work. By reviewing what you have done, you can improve weak points that otherwise would be missed. Read and reread your paper.

- Does it make logical sense?
  Leave it for a few hours and then read it again. Does it still make logical sense?
- Do the sentences flow smoothly from one another? If not, try to add some words and phrases to help connect them. Transition words, such as "therefore" or "however," sometimes help. Also, you might refer in one sentence to a thought in the previous sentence. This is especially useful when you move from one paragraph to another.
- Have you run a spell checker or a grammar checker? These aids cannot catch every error, but they might catch errors that you have missed.

Once you have checked your work and perfected your formatting, your essay is finished.

Congratulations!

102 *Little Red Book of Essay Writing*

Introduction Paragraph

What is an introduction paragraph?

The introduction paragraph is the first paragraph of your essay.

What does it do?

It introduces the main idea of your essay. A good opening paragraph captures the interest of your reader and tells why your topic is important.

How do I write one?

1. Write the thesis statement. The main idea of the essay is stated in a single sentence called the thesis statement. You must limit your entire essay to the topic you have introduced in your thesis statement.
2. Provide some background information about your topic. You can use interesting facts, quotations, or definitions of important terms you will use later in the essay.

Example: Hockey has been a part of life in Canada for over 120 years. It has evolved into an extremely popular sport watched and played by millions of Canadians. The game has gone through several changes since hockey was first played in Canada.

Supporting Paragraphs

What are supporting paragraphs?

Supporting paragraphs make up the main body of your essay.

What do they do?

They develop the main idea of your essay.

How do I write them?

1. List the points that develop the main idea of your essay.
2. Place each supporting point in its own paragraph.

Little Red Book of Essay Writing **103**

3. Develop each supporting point with facts, details, and examples.

To connect your supporting paragraphs, you should use special transition words. Transition words link your paragraphs together and make your essay easier to read. Use them at the beginning and end of your paragraphs.

Examples of transition words that can help you to link your paragraphs together:

For listing different points
First
Second
Third

For additional ideas
Another
In addition to
Related to
Furthermore
Also

For counter examples
However
Even though
On the other hand
Nevertheless

To show cause and effect
Therefore
Thus
As a result of
Consequently

Like all good paragraphs, each supporting paragraph should have a topic sentence, supporting sentences, and a summary sentence.

Essay Menu

Summary Paragraph

What is a summary paragraph?
The summary paragraph comes at the end of your essay after you have finished developing your ideas. The summary paragraph is often called a "conclusion."

104 *Little Red Book of Essay Writing*

What does it do?

It summarizes or restates the main idea of the essay. You want to leave the reader with a sense that your essay is complete.

How do I write one?

1. Restate the strongest points of your essay that support your main idea.
2. Conclude your essay by restating the main idea in different words.
3. Give your personal opinion or suggest a plan for action.

Example: Overall, the changes that occurred in hockey have helped to improve the game. Hockey is faster and more exciting as a result of changes in the past 120 years. For these reasons, modern hockey is a better game than hockey in the 1890s.

Prewriting Essays

What is the prewriting stage?

The prewriting stage when you prepare your ideas for your essay before you begin writing. You will find it easier to write your essay if you build an outline first, especially when you are writing longer assignments.

Six Prewriting Steps

1. **Think carefully about what you are going to write.** Ask yourself: What question am I going to answer in this paragraph or essay? How can I best answer this question? What is the most important part of my answer? How can I make an introductory sentence (or thesis statement) from the most important part of my answer? What facts or ideas can I use to support my introductory

Little Red Book of Essay Writing **105**

sentence? How can I make this paragraph or essay interesting? Do I need more facts on this topic? Where can I find more facts on this topic?

2. **Open your notebook.** Write out your answers to the above questions. You do not need to spend a lot of time doing this; just write enough to help you remember why and how you are going to write your paragraph or essay.

3. **Collect facts related to your paragraph or essay topic.** Look for and write down facts that will help you to answer your question. Timesaving hint: make sure the facts you are writing are related to the exact question you are going to answer in your paragraph or essay.

4. **Write down your own ideas.** Ask yourself: What else do I want to say about this topic? Why should people be interested in this topic? Why is this topic important?

5. **Find the main idea of your paragraph or essay.** Choose the most important point you are going to present. If you cannot decide which point is the most important, just choose one point and stick to it throughout your paragraph or essay.

6. **Organize your facts and ideas in a way that develops your main idea.** Once you have chosen the most important point of your paragraph or essay, you must find the best way to tell your reader about it. Look at the facts you have written. Look at your own ideas on the topic. Decide which facts and ideas will best support the main idea of your essay. Once you have chosen the facts and ideas you plan to use, ask yourself which order to put them in the essay. Write down your own note set that you can use to guide yourself as you write your essay.

106 *Little Red Book of Essay Writing*

Writing Essays

What is the writing stage?
The writing stage is when you turn your ideas into sentences.

Five Writing Steps:

1. For the introduction, write the thesis statement and give some background information.
2. Develop each supporting paragraph and make sure to follow the correct paragraph format.
3. Write clear and simple sentences to express your meaning.
4. Focus on the main idea of your essay.
5. Use a dictionary to help you find additional words to express your meaning.

Editing Essays

What is the editing stage?
The editing stage is when you check your essay for mistakes and correct them.

Editing Steps

Grammar and Spelling
1. Check your spelling.
2. Check your grammar.
3. Read your essay again.
4. Make sure each sentence has a subject.
5. Make sure your subjects and verbs agree with each other.
6. Check the verb tenses of each sentence.
7. Make sure that each sentence makes sense.

Style and Organization
1. Make sure your essay has an introduction, supporting paragraphs, and a summary paragraph.

Little Red Book of Essay Writing **107**

2. Check that you have a thesis statement that identifies the main idea of the essay.
3. Check that all your paragraphs follow the proper paragraph format.
4. See if your essay is interesting.

Definition Essay

When you are writing a definition essay, you take a term or an idea and write about what it is. Often, definitions are combined with classification or other forms of organization in the essay. You need to give a careful definition of the key term before going on to discuss different types or examples.

Example question:	Write an essay defining energy resources and discuss the different types.
Introduction:	Define the key term energy resources.
Supporting paragraphs:	1. *Define one type of energy resources:* renewable resources.
	2. *Define another type of energy resources:* non-renewable resources.
Summary paragraph:	Summarize energy resources.

Classification Essay

In a classification essay, you separate things or ideas into specific categories and discuss each of them. You organize the essay by defining each classification and by giving examples of each type.

108 *Little Red Book of Essay Writing*

Example question:	Write an essay discussing the three types of government in Canada.
Introduction:	Give background information about government in Canada.
Supporting paragraphs:	1. Define and describe federal government.
	2. Define and describe provincial governments.
	3. Define and describe municipal governments.
Summary paragraph:	Summarize government in Canada.

Description Essay

In a description essay, you write about what a person, place, or thing is like. You organize the essay by describing different parts or aspects of the main subject.

Example question:	Write an essay describing the polar bear.
Introduction:	Introduce what a polar bear is.
Supporting paragraphs:	1. Describe where the polar bear lives.
	2. Describe the body of the polar bear.
	3. Describe what the polar eats.
Summary paragraph:	Summarize what a polar bear is.

Compare and Contrast Essay

In a compare and contrast essay, you write about the similarities and differences between two or more people,

Little Red Book of Essay Writing **109**

places, or things. You can organize the essay by writing about one subject first and then comparing it with the second subject. A more effective way is to organize the essay by comparing each subject by category.

Example:	Write an essay comparing the weather in Vancouver and Halifax.
Introduction:	Introduce weather in the cities of Vancouver and Halifax.
Supporting paragraphs:	1. Compare weather in spring and summer for both cities. State how they are similar or different.
	2. Compare weather in fall and winter for both cities. State how they are similar or different
Summary paragraph:	Summarize the similarities and differences.

Sequence Essay

In a sequence essay, you are writing to describe a series of events or a process in some sort of order. Usually, this order is based on time. You organize the essay by writing about each step of the process in the order it occurred.

Example question:	Write an essay outlining the stages of the salmon life cycle.
Introduction:	Describe what a salmon is like.
Supporting paragraphs:	1. Describe young salmon.
	2. Describe adult salmon.

110 *Little Red Book of Essay Writing*

	3. Describe what salmon do before they die.
Summary paragraph:	Summarize the main steps of the salmon life cycle.

Choice Essay

In a choice essay, you need to choose which object, idea, or action that you prefer. You organize the essay by describing each option and then giving your opinion.

Example question:	Write an essay choosing between hockey in the 1890s and hockey today.
Introduction:	Introduce the game of hockey.
Supporting paragraphs:	1. Describe hockey in the 1890s.
	2. Describe hockey today.
	3. State which form of hockey you prefer and why.
Summary paragraph:	Summarize the game of hockey.

Explanation Essay

In an explanation essay, you explain how or why something happens or has happened. You need to explain different causes and effects. You should organize the essay by explaining each individual cause or effect.

Example question:	Write an essay explaining why so many Europeans moved to Canada during the early nineteenth century.
Introduction:	Give background information on European immigration during this time.

Little Red Book of Essay Writing **111**

Supporting paragraphs:	1.	Explain first reason: poor economy in Europe.
	2.	Explain second reason: better living conditions in Canada.
Summary paragraph:		Summarize main reasons.

Evaluation Essay

In an evaluation essay, you make judgments about people, ideas, and possible actions. You make your evaluation based on certain criteria that you develop. Organize the essay by discussing the criteria you used to make your judgement.

Example question:		Write an essay evaluating the importance of the House of Commons.
Introduction:		Give your judgement on whether the House of Commons is important.
Supporting paragraphs:	1.	Explain first criteria: meeting place for government
	2.	Explain second criteria: represent Canadians
	3.	Explain third criteria: make laws for Canada
Summary paragraph:		Conclude with an overall judgement about the House of Commons

Essays Parts

Parts of an Essay

Introduction
Supporting Paragraphs
Summary Paragraph

112   *Little Red Book of Essay Writing*

How to Write an Essay	Prewriting Essays
	Writing Essays
	Editing Essays
	Publishing Essays
Kinds of Essays	Definition
	Classification
	Description
Compare and Contrast	Sequence
	Choice
	Explanation
	Evaluation

How To Write An Essay: 10 Easy Steps

Writing is making sense of life.

— Nadine Gordimer

Why is writing an essay so frustrating?

Learning how to write an essay can be a maddening, exasperating process, but it doesn't have to be. If you know the steps and understand what to do, writing can be easy and even fun.

This site, "How To Write an Essay: 10 Easy Steps," offers a ten-step process that teaches students how to write an essay. Links to the writing steps are found on the left, and additional writing resources are located across the top.

Learning how to write an essay doesn't have to involve so much trial and error.

Brief Overview of the 10 Essay Writing Steps

Below are brief summaries of each of the ten steps to writing an essay. Select the links for more info on any particular step, or use the blue navigation bar on the left to proceed through the writing steps. *How To Write an Essay* can be

Little Red Book of Essay Writing **113**

viewed sequentially, as if going through ten sequential steps in an essay writing process, or can be explored by individual topic:

1. **Research:** Begin the essay writing process by researching your topic, making yourself an expert. Utilize the internet, the academic databases, and the library. Take notes and immerse yourself in the words of great thinkers.

2. **Analysis:** Now that you have a good knowledge base, start analyzing the arguments of the essays you're reading. Clearly define the claims, write out the reasons, the evidence. Look for weaknesses of logic, and also strengths. Learning how to write an essay begins by learning how to analyze essays written by others.

3. **Brainstorming:** Your essay will require insight of your own, genuine essay-writing brilliance. Ask yourself a dozen questions and answer them. Meditate with a pen in your hand. Take walks and think and think until you come up with original insights to write about.

4. **Thesis:** Pick your best idea and pin it down in a clear assertion that you can write your entire essay around. Your thesis is your main point, summed up in a concise sentence that lets the reader know where you're going, and why. It's practically impossible to write a good essay without a clear thesis.

5. **Outline:** Sketch out your essay before straightway writing it out. Use one-line sentences to describe paragraphs, and bullet points to describe what each paragraph will contain. Play with the essay's order. Map out the structure of your argument, and make sure each paragraph is unified.

114 *Little Red Book of Essay Writing*

6. **Introduction:** Now sit down and write the essay. The introduction should grab the reader's attention, set up the issue, and lead in to your thesis. Your intro is merely a buildup of the issue, a stage of bringing your reader into the essay's argument.

   NOTE: The title and first paragraph are probably the most important elements in your essay. This is an essay-writing point that doesn't always sink in within the context of the classroom. In the first paragraph you either hook the reader's interest or lose it. Of course your teacher, who's getting paid to teach you how to write an essay, will read the essay you've written regardless, but in the real world, readers make up their minds about whether or not to read your essay by glancing at the title alone.

7. **Paragraphs:** Each individual paragraph should be focused on a single idea that supports your thesis. Begin paragraphs with topic sentences, support assertions with evidence, and expound your ideas in the clearest, most sensible way you can. Speak to your reader as if he or she were sitting in front of you. In other words, instead of writing the essay, try *talking* the essay.

8. **Conclusion:** Gracefully exit your essay by making a quick wrap-up sentence, and then end on some memorable thought, perhaps a quotation, or an interesting twist of logic, or some call to action. Is there something you want the reader to walk away and do? Let him or her know exactly what.

9. **MLA Style:** Format your essay according to the correct guidelines for citation. All borrowed ideas and quotations should be correctly cited in the body of your text,

Little Red Book of Essay Writing **115**

followed up with a Works Cited (references) page listing the details of your sources.

10. **Language:** You're not done writing your essay until you've polished your language by correcting the grammar, making sentences flow, incoporating rhythm, emphasis, adjusting the formality, giving it a level-headed tone, and making other intuitive edits. Proofread until it reads just how you want it to sound. Writing an essay can be tedious, but you don't want to bungle the hours of conceptual work you've put into writing your essay by leaving a few slippymisppallings and pourly worded phrazies.

NOTE: You're done. Great job. Now move over Ernest Hemingway—a new writer is coming of age! (*Of course Hemingway was a fiction writer, not an essay writer, but he probably knew how to write an essay just as well.*)

My Promise: The Rest of This Site Will Really Teach You How To Write an Essay

For half a dozen years I've read thousands of college essays and taught students how to write essays, do research, analyze arguments, and so on. I wrote this site in the most basic, practical way possible and made the instruction crystal clear for students and instructors to follow. If you carefully follow the ten steps for writing an essay as outlined on this site — honestly and carefully follow them — you'll learn how to write an essay that is more organized, insightful, and appealing. And you'll probably get an A.

116 *Little Red Book of Essay Writing*

Now it's time to really begin. Come on, it will be fun. I promise to walk you through each step of your writing journey.

11. **Step 1:** Research

12. Assuming you've been given a topic, or have narrowed it sufficiently down, your first task is to research this topic. You will not be able to write intelligently about a topic you know nothing about. To discover worthwhile insights, you'll have to do some patient reading.

13. Read light sources, then thorough

14. When you conduct research, move from light to thorough resources to make sure you're moving in the right direction. Begin by doing searches on the Internet about your topic to familiarize yourself with the basic issues; then move to more thorough research on the Academic Databases; finally, probe the depths of the issue by burying yourself in the library. Make sure that despite beginning on the Internet, you don't simply end there. A research paper using only Internet sources is a weak paper, and puts you at a disadvantage for not utilizing better information from more academic sources.

15. Write down quotations

16. As you read about your topic, keep a piece of paper and pen handy to write down interesting quotations you find. Make sure you write down the source and transcribe quotations accurately. I recommend handwriting the quotations to ensure that you don't overuse them, because if you have to handwrite the quotations, you'll probably only use quotations sparingly, as you should. On the other hand, if you're cruising through the net,

Little Red Book of Essay Writing **117**

you may just want to cut and paste snippets here and there *along with their URLs* into a Word file, and then later go back and sift the kernels from the chaff.